Morning
Glory

Based on the motion picture
written by Aline Brosh McKenna

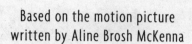

Morning
Glory

A Novel by
Diana Peterfreund

BALLANTINE BOOKS TRADE PAPERBACKS
NEW YORK

A Ballantine Books Trade Paperback Original

Copyright © 2010 by Paramount Pictures Corporation

Published in the United States by Ballantine Books, an imprint of The Random House Publishing Group, a division of Random House, Inc., New York.

BALLANTINE and colophon are registered trademarks of Random House, Inc.

ISBN 978-0-345-52393-8

Printed in the United States of America

2 4 6 8 9 7 5 3 1

Book design by Liz Cosgrove

Morning Glory

The restaurant seemed designed for a first date. The tables were covered with white cloths, but the rest of the decor wasn't overly twee. The menu had enough trendy items to mark the chef as with the times, and enough old favorites to please the fussiest of eaters. The Zagat sticker on the door made it seem dependable. It came across as elegant and fun, which would hopefully reflect the same attributes onto the person—me—who'd chosen the spot. In fact, there was only one problem with the restaurant.

It was closed.

I knocked politely on the glass door. "Hello?" I called. The bartender looked up from polishing the stemware. I pointed at my watch. "Your website says you open at four thirty."

He flipped the lock and opened the door for me. "Are you the new hostess?"

I blinked at him. "No. Becky Fuller. Table for two at four thirty."

"I haven't even checked the reservation list yet," he said with a shrug. "You can come in, but there's no way we can seat you for another ten minutes or so." He peered around me, then fixed me with an appraising look. "Where's your number two?"

I frowned, feeling defensive. Didn't I look like someone who could get a date? Even a 4:30 date? "He'll be here soon." I checked my watch again. "It's only . . . four fifteen."

The bartender smirked. "That I know." Was he flirting with me? Not particularly adept flirting, maybe, but I was hardly one to talk. Also, a little awkward, what with me actually waiting for a date.

Inside, I folded myself into the tiny window seat near the coat check and whipped out my BlackBerry.

"Can I get you a glass of wine?" the bartender called across the empty restaurant. I was beginning to suspect he was, if not the owner, at least the manager of the restaurant. Why else would he be here all alone?

"I'm fine for now," I replied, my thumbs moving furiously on the keyboard.

After a minute, he spoke again. "Do I know you?"

I glanced up. I didn't think I knew him. Not bad-looking, about my age, or maybe a few years older. Slightly receding hairline, with the corresponding close-cropped cut that guys with receding hairlines liked nowadays.

Actually, that might be a good story. "Why Bald's Not Bad." Or maybe something more positive-sounding. Tie it into bald celebrities. Bruce Willis. Vin Diesel. Not that we ever lacked for trend pieces. It was real news stories that tripped us up.

"Becky Fuller," he mused. "Wait, did you go to Fairleigh Dickinson?"

My thumbs stopped and I peered at him again. "Yes."

"Me too," he said, though my mind still drew a blank. "Ben Smith."

Nothing. And the common name didn't help. Did I go out with him? I tried to picture him with hair.

"Maybe you'd remember my boyfriend," Ben Smith went on. Okay, so *not* flirting. Man, I was bad at reading signals. Epically bad. We'd done a piece two months ago on face blindness? People who couldn't recognize their children, their husbands, their own faces in the mirror? Well, I clearly had flirt blindness.

And probably hadn't dated him either. Though college was a long time ago, and with my track record, I wouldn't be surprised if there'd been a few gay guys on the list. "His name is Steve Jones?"

Steve Jones and Ben Smith. Unlikely. I could name every member of the Hoboken City Council for the last five years. My BlackBerry listed the phone number of the dean of every institute of higher learning from Berkeley to William Paterson. I could rattle off the stats of every New Jersey athlete drafted by a professional sports team since the turn of the millennium. Unless Steve Jones was one of these people, I didn't know him.

"You dropped out, though," he went on. "What happened?"

I lowered my BlackBerry and hesitated over whether or not to spill my life story to a restaurant manager I did not remember who'd apparently attended the college I'd dropped out of. Usually, I was the one around here doing the interviews.

The door to the restaurant opened and in walked my date. I shoved my BlackBerry into my jacket pocket and popped up to meet him.

"Becky?" He smiled. Nice smile.

I smiled at Ben in triumph. See? There *was* a number two. "It's a long story," I said, as he grudgingly grabbed a pair of menus to show us to our seats.

Why had I dropped out of Fairleigh? I'd had a better offer.

Six minutes later, I wondered if I'd have been better off having that glass of wine with Ben after all. It was now officially 4:30, so the restaurant was officially open and we could, I supposed, officially order. That was, if the waitress ever finished her staff meal and got her butt over here.

Also, in six minutes, my BlackBerry had gone off in my jacket pocket no fewer than four times, and it was taking all my concentration not to answer its siren's call. Focus I should have been using to make up for all the elegance and fun that this restaurant apparently didn't have at 4:30.

Ben Smith had departed to points unknown, which lessened the pressure I felt to reminisce with him about vaguely remembered school days. Though that conversation might have been easier than the one I was trying and failing to keep going with my actual date.

"I'm just glad you were able to meet me so early," I said, trying not to toy with my silverware. "I know it's a pain. . . ."

"Oh, that's okay," said my date. "I've . . . never been to dinner at this time. Interesting crowd."

Interesting indeed. In one corner of the restaurant, a duo of octogenarians were squinting at the menu from behind their bifocals. In another, two waiters and a busboy were finishing up their staff meals.

I forced a smile. "Professional hazard. See, I work at *Good Morning New Jersey*—"

"On Channel 9, right?" he replied. His name was Jon, but not, I'd discovered, Jon-short-for-Jonathan, which was a little confusing. My downstairs neighbor had set this up. Jon worked in her office. New in town. The usual.

"Exactly, and we're on really early, so I've got a bedtime like a toddler." Why not just John? I was Becky, not Beccie or Beki or anything weird. Once people started getting creative with the spelling, things always went wrong on the prompters. Well, it would be fine with Jon, but still—

My BlackBerry began to buzz again. I could feel it purring in my jacket pocket. I know it sounds crazy, but I think I've developed a sixth sense about these things. This was a particularly desperate purr.

"Sorry, I have to—" I pulled it out and checked. "I'm working on a story about the mosquito infestation in Ho-Ho-Kus near the . . ." I read the email and grimaced. Did Anna think I was freaking Wikipedia? I glanced up at Jon. "Do mosquitoes bite or sting?"

"Not sure," Jon said. "But when I lived there, I was pretty sure the Ho-Ho-Kus mosquitoes used martial arts."

Cute. He was cute. And patient. I rushed through my email—I went with "bite," for the record—and set the Black-Berry down on the tabletop. "Okay, done and done."

"So," Jon said, his eyes glinting. "You were talking about your bedtime?"

Well played, sir. But I remained cool. "Well, we used to be on at five A.M., but then the station got bought by this giant company and they decided to run us instead of infomercials since we generate slightly more revenue, so we start at four A.M. now."

"Bummer."

The BlackBerry went off again, skittering across the table like an electronic cockroach. I grabbed it.

"Let me just . . . ," I said as Jon gave me a raised eyebrow over the top of the menu. Right—once was a pass. "I'll turn it off."

As soon as I checked the readout, that is. Oh, crap. Anna.

"So sorry," I said to Jon, as I pressed the phone to my ear. "This will just be two seconds—hi."

"Becky," Anna's voice came on the line. "I don't mean to interrupt, but please tell me you got that last email."

"He confirmed for tomorrow," I said. "I sent you the list of questions."

Jon flipped a page in the menu. Desserts? Really? But we hadn't even ordered.

"And do we have any—," Anna went on.

"I already pulled the footage from the Weehawken mosquito investigation two years ago. Okaygottagobye! Wear bug spray!" I hung up, turned back to Jon, and smiled in apology. "I know, it's so annoying when people do that. You just want to go, 'Check please.'"

"No—," Jon said.

"It's just that it's a kind of 'round-the-clock job, you know? Even at the local station. I mean, we're nothing special, it's not like we're the *Today* show. They're the gold standard."

"Really—," Jon said.

"Yeah, if you think about it. And we're just . . . anyway, sorry about that. I won't touch it again."

Jon looked skeptical. Crap.

"This place is nice, huh?" I tried. "It reminds me of Matthews, in Waldwick? We used to go there when I was a kid."

"Not familiar—," Jon said.

"I always had the Belgian waffles," I went on, helpless to stop myself. Not only was I flirt-blind, I was apparently also banter-impaired. No wonder I liked to stay *behind* the camera. "Then my dad died when I was nine, and my mom moved to Florida five years ago for her phlebitis—apparently, blood clots differently in Florida. . . ."

Jon was staring at me, clearly as flummoxed by my babbling as I was.

"Anyway," I said, getting control of my mouth. "What do you do?"

He hesitated for a second. "I'm in marketing. For an insurance company."

"Oh," I said, as gamely as possible. "That's . . . nice."

The BlackBerry began to do its insect impression again, making a trembling dash for the table edge. I caught it in midair.

"Oh my God, this is my boss. I have to—"

Jon opened his menu again.

"I could . . . call him back."

He flipped to the "About Our Chef" page, the last refuge of the truly bored. "No, no. Go ahead."

"Really?" I beamed. "It'll just be a second, I promise." I slid from my chair and answered. This had better be worth it— Jon was growing increasingly restless.

"All I want to know, Becky," said Oscar, "is that you got that CEO."

I cast a glance back at Jon, who was watching the octogenarians squabbling over whether to order the beet salad or the grilled radicchio. Perhaps he was envying their companionable vibes. Damn, I was bad at dating.

"I left three messages with his attorney," I said. "And if he doesn't call back, I'll just wait outside his office."

It was way easier to nail down stories than dates.

Jon signaled to the waiter. "Check please."

Way easier.

My eyes popped open as soon as the alarm went off: 1:30 A.M. Another day. I reached for the remote controlling the dresser TV. *Good morning, CNN.*

I flicked on the TV on my bookshelf. *Guten tag, MSNBC.*

And the one gracing the storage chest at the end of the bed. *Okay, FOX News. This is your last chance. Show me some love or I'm trading you out for C-SPAN. I mean it this time.*

I brushed my teeth, keeping one eye on the state of my gums and the other on the reflection of the bookshelf TV in my bathroom mirror. A whole lot of nothing this morning. The other producers better have come through with that mosquito stuff, especially since they'd ruined my date with Jon.

He'd been a cute one, too. Given my hours, it was rare to meet someone outside the field of night security or newspaper delivery. There'd been that nice baker from Hoboken two years back, but I'd put on fifteen pounds while dating him. I hadn't eaten like that since leaving college.

A breaking news bar flashed on the CNN screen. I whirled, toothbrush and all, to catch the details. Wait . . . a car accident in Phoenix? Never mind. They certainly had a broad definition of the term "news" down there in Atlanta.

I got dressed, grabbed my computer case, my purse, my

tote bag with my gym stuff, my other tote bag with my folders on developing stories, and my jacket. As I shoved the key into the lock on my door, I passed Jim, my neighbor, who was clearly just returning from taking his Puggle to piddle.

"Night, Jim," I said, making a wide berth around his yapping dog.

"Morning, Becky," he replied.

And that's my life. Dinner dates at 4 P.M., in bed by eight, up at 1:30 A.M. and ready to share important news stories with the world.

On a perfect day, that is. Sometimes what's important ends up being more about the best places to buy organic chicken than actual hard-hitting journalism. But who is to say that poultry info isn't utterly relevant to the housewife in Edgewater? There's no law that says all news should be about Yemen or North Korea.

In the car, I started flipping stations. Soft rock, advertisements, a Christian call-in show . . . ah, news. Weather, traffic, got it covered, covered it yesterday, wait . . . what did Kim Kardashian wear? Hmmm. Maybe worth a trend piece?

Nah. Not another one of those. Someone give me some real news. *Talk to me, NPR.*

I stopped to pick up the newspapers and pulled into the Channel 9 parking lot.

My friend and coproducer, Anna Garcia, pounced on me as soon as I was inside. I hoped it wasn't more questions about mosquitoes.

"So? How was the date?"

A few years younger than me, Anna had the benefit of still thinking every blind date had the potential of being The One. It was easier to do so when you were Anna Garcia, though. She had the face of an angel and a knack for serial monogamy. In the entire time I'd known her, she'd never been single for more than a month, total.

Perhaps I should lie and spin her a marvelous tale about my epic evening. Maybe I should tell her I didn't get home until some ungodly hour . . . like 9 P.M.

"Pretty good," I said. "He was nice. We, um, kind of hit it off." Or we did until I started checking my BlackBerry every two seconds like a crazy.

Anna regarded me skeptically. "Did you check your Black-Berry every two seconds like a crazy?"

"Yes," I admitted. "But I did it in an adorable way."

Anna smirked. Yeah, I didn't buy it either.

2

At the staff meeting, I stared across the table at the usual sea of bleary eyes. Some people, you see, are better at adhering to our established work schedules than others. While I scheduled dinner dates in order to catch the early-bird specials, some of my coworkers still acted like they were on spring break in Barcelona. Take Sam, for instance. Sam was probably up late last night watching the game. Didn't matter what game. If it could by any stretch of the imagination be called a sport—from football to synchronized swimming to canine agility—Sam was all over it. Ironically, he couldn't so much as dribble a basketball himself, which was an ongoing disappointment to anyone who was ever looking for a pickup game or an office league, as Sam was six-foot-five. On the plus side, he could always be counted on to fill out our schedule with sports stories. I wondered how long Sam would last at Channel 9. He was too good for this show.

And I liked to think he wasn't alone there.

"Becky?" said my boss, Oscar. "Why don't you start us out with what you've got."

I slid out my latest file. "There's a state spelling bee champion—"

"Spelling bee?" one of the other producers asked dubiously.

Oh, just you wait. "A *deaf* spelling bee champ," I clarified. "She's deaf, see? And so she can't hear the word, so they sign it to her in ASL, and then she *finger-spells* it for them. It's a great story."

Oscar looked unmoved. "But if she's signing, and it's a spelling bee, how can the audience tell if she's right?"

Bingo. I smiled. "She has a brother. He translates."

Oscar nodded once.

And I hadn't gotten to the really good part yet. "He has a lisp."

Oscar's eyes lit up.

"You'll cry," I promised. Everyone would. I saw Daytime Emmys flash before Oscar's face.

"Sounds terrific," said Oscar. "Go for it. Now, who's working on this Board of Education thing?"

I piped up again. "They're having a meeting on the eighth. I'm going down there. Looks like there could be some firings in Newark."

"Great." Oscar turned to Sam. "And how's it going for the horse race remote on Tuesday?"

"We're all set," I said at the same time as Sam.

Oscar raised his eyebrows.

Sam shrugged. "I, uh, asked Becky to help out since she's done so many of these."

"We're renting a mini-rig," I said. "It's cheaper and we can get close to the action. I was even thinking we could get someone in the winner's circle and—"

"That's a great idea!" said Sam. He loved winner's circles. "But how would we—"

"We'll just get the crew to duck under the ropes, and then try to nab an interview with the winning jockey."

"Or the horse," said Anna under her breath.

I kicked her beneath the table.

After the meeting, I dropped by the studio control room to check on the broadcast. Channel 9 was not what you'd call the cutting edge of commercial broadcasting. The set decor was a little too *Mad Men* for my taste. However, since we hadn't updated in half a century, I supposed we could enjoy the perks of being retro-chic.

Behind our anchor, Ralph, I could see a strip of paint peeling right off the backdrop.

Was there such a thing as *shabby* retro-chic?

Ralph was another relic. He'd been doing the broadcast here for at least five sets of toupees, if the hair and makeup records were to be believed. He was also solid as a rock, and said things like:

"Good morning, New Jersey, it's four thirty-eight A.M."

As if it was the first 4:38 A.M. he'd ever announced on air, instead of the four thousandth.

"Taking a quick look at traffic," Ralph was saying, "the Holland Tunnel is still backed up due to an overturned big rig in the right-hand lane. Officials say it should be cleared up within the hour. . . ."

His coanchor, Louanne, was another story. Things hadn't been the same at the show since she gave birth to those twins eight months ago. I yearned for the time baby Oliver and baby Madelyn would start sleeping through the night. More sleep for them meant less sleep—*on-set* sleep—for Louanne. Speaking of which . . .

"Oh, Jesus, not again." She was catnapping on-screen. Or wait—what had her doctor called it after her last performance review? Microsleeping, right. Whatever.

I whispered to the director, "Go to a single on Ralph." I pressed the button for the stage manager's earpiece. "Fred," I said. "Look lively."

Louanne's head started to tilt sideways.

". . . But until then," Ralph was saying, "expect delays from Ridgefield Park to Route 78. And that's a look at the traffic and weather. Coming up next, we'll be talking to an expert who says the vitamins in our medicine cabinets may be filled with toxins. Join us for an inside look at the hidden dangers in your own home."

A pad of Post-it notes zinged across the desk, thwapping Louanne squarely in the side of the head. She jerked awake.

Fred stood at the edge of the set, a pencil in one hand and an apple in the other, ready to fire off those missiles next if the Post-it warning shot didn't do the job.

Suitably chastened, Louanne smiled at the camera. "All that and a look at sports at the top of the hour."

I shook my head and pressed the earpiece button again. "Nice shot, Fred. You're a stud."

A stud who'd probably done the sixties paint job himself. The grizzled Fred gave me a grin and juggled the apple and pencil. "No problemo."

Anna waved me over from the weather station, and I met her just as the very white Harold the Hip-Hop Meteorologist went into his spiel.

"The rain will fall, when you go to the mall, bring an um-brella, and a jacket for your fella. . . ."

Anna winced. "Really, with this guy?"

I lifted my shoulders. "People love him."

"Later it will clear, warmer it will feel . . . ," Harold rapped. Lord knew why, but people *did* love him.

"I'm people," Anna grumbled. "I don't. And 'clear' does not rhyme with 'feel.'"

"It's assonance." I cocked my head at Harold as he warned our viewers about canceling their duck hunt due to the approaching cold front.

"And 'Warmer it will feel'?" Anna said. "He's been getting a little Yoda lately."

I sighed. "People love Yoda, too."

"So," said Anna, "did you hear they got the budget approved to move someone up?"

I completely lost track of the weatherman's rhyme scheme. "What? How do you know that?"

"I talked to Raymond in HR." Raymond in HR would do anything for Anna. Raymond in HR didn't seem to realize that Anna would only date him after an international pandemic rid the world of 98 percent of the male population. Raymond in HR was actually pretty cute, but he'd probably only date *me* if an international pandemic rid the world of 98 percent of the *female* population. This was due to a long-standing argument we had over my refusal to hire anyone he sent me who called it "Alannic City."

"He said the company is reorganizing all the stations and they've budgeted *us* for a senior producer."

Harold the Hip-Hop Meteorologist could have finally found a rhyme for South Orange and I wouldn't have noticed in that moment. "Wait a second," I said. "Are you sure?"

Anna grinned. "He said they pulled your employment records. You're getting it, Becky. You're finally getting The Job."

The Job. The one I'd wanted ever since leaving Fairleigh Dickinson for Channel 9. My own show. My own studio. Senior Producer of *Good Morning, New Jersey.* My very own kingdom. Or queendom. Or something. Oh my God.

I floated back to the cameras near the head desk. My head desk. My cameras. Maybe I could get the set repainted. I wondered how much of a raise I was looking at. Not much, given our microscopic budget, but still.

Louanne's caffeine pill seemed to have kicked in. "Police say the dog was stolen from the pet store while workers were cleaning the cages."

Of course, with stories like that to report, it was little wonder she was falling asleep.

"The puppy, a Chinese Crested, is worth over six hundred dollars and answers to the name 'Manchu.' "

There was another change I could make once I was the executive producer. Better stories, with more substance.

Oscar came over as I watched the broadcast with an eye toward improvements. "Hey, Becky. Can you come by my office right after the show?"

I tried my best to radiate surprise. "What? Me? Yes, of course."

I turned to the monitors, trying to catch my reflection. Was my hair mussed? Was there lipstick on my teeth? I wanted to look as nice as possible for the The Moment When I Got The Job. If only my dad had lived to see this day. When I was little, we used to sit and watch the evening news together every night. My father and me and on the TV, Mike Pomeroy, the old IBS evening news anchor. As far as Dad and

I were concerned, he was the best news anchor of all time. Too bad he wasn't on the air anymore.

In the hallway on my way to the office, I was stopped and accosted by Anna and some of the other producers.

"Wait a minute, Becky," Anna said, shoving a gift bag at me. "We thought you might need this."

I poked at the tissue paper coming out of the top. "This had better not be a box of condoms again. I still have the old one." I opened the bag and pulled out a T-shirt. Huge block letters across the front read I ACCEPT!

"Awww, guys. This is so sweet."

"Put it on," Anna coaxed.

"No," I said, and balled the T-shirt up again. "I can't. That would be too weird."

"Come on," said Anna. "We're proud of you. And we just hope that when you're a big superstar someday at the *Today* show, you'll still answer our emails."

I laughed. The *Today* show? Not likely. But I'd take *Good Morning, New Jersey* and be happy with it.

"Come on," Anna repeated. "Oscar will love it."

I laughed and headed to the bathroom. From behind me, I heard one of the other producers whisper to Anna, "She *is* going to get it, right?"

"Oh, Jesus, I hope so" was Anna's reply.

I decided to send up a prayer of my own.

Oscar had the nicest office at Channel 9. Actually, Oscar had the only office at Channel 9, while the rest of us managed with cubicles. I wondered if, now that they'd budgeted for a senior producer, they'd also budget for a senior producer's office. There was that empty supply closet on the second floor.

No windows, but I could see repurposing it. I started to bounce, then stopped myself. Cool. Calm. And professional.

I tugged my blazer closed over the T-shirt Anna had made me wear and stepped inside.

Oscar was seated at his desk, and he looked up as I entered. "Becky . . ."

"That's me," I squeaked, then got ahold of myself. "I mean, you know that. Never mind, I—" I plopped down on the chair across from him and took several deep breaths. *Try to look like a senior producer, you moron.*

Oscar didn't seem to notice my flub. "You're a terrific producer, you know that, right?"

"Well, I try," I said awkwardly. Of course *I* knew it. The question was, did *he*? And was he willing to recognize it?

"Yes, you do," he said. "You really, really do. And you've been here a long time. You started as an intern when you were what?"

"Seventeen," I pointed out. Company loyalty. Dependability. Experience. Dedication. Vote for Becky Fuller for Senior Producer!

"Seventeen." Oscar shook his head in disbelief. Exactly. You didn't see that kind of long-standing relationship these days. I was Channel 9—born and bred. "And you've always been outstanding."

I nodded my head demurely. "Thank you."

He was silent for a moment, no doubt wishing to draw out the anticipation of The Moment When I Got The Job. I gave him my most encouraging smile, the one I used on reluctant interview subjects. He stood up and walked over to the window.

I straightened in my seat and undid the buttons on my blazer. Oscar would get a kick out of this. We'd laugh about it at his retirement party in ten years. It would pass into Channel 9 lore. The Senior Producer Who Accepted Her New Job Via T-shirt. *I ACCEPT!*

"And you see, Becky," Oscar was saying, still facing the window.

Here it comes. Here it comes. I opened my arms. Ta-da! *I ACCEPT!*

"We have to let you go."

I ACC—I gasped. What? *No.* That wasn't what he was supposed to say. I hugged my blazer closed around myself.

"I'm really sorry, Becky—" Oscar turned around and saw me struggling to close my blazer around the T-shirt. "What are you—"

"I . . ." I choked. "I don't understand."

Oscar began speaking very quickly. "Corporate wants us to reduce our overhead. We're making big cuts."

Big . . . oh, God.

"And they want me to hire a senior producer with more business experience to manage the contraction of the show. Even though it means we can't afford everyone."

The contraction of the show? Of *my* show? I wasn't being promoted? I was being . . . *contracted?*

Why didn't that mean what it sounded like?

I tried to breathe, but it came out more like a gulp. "But you told them you can't do that, right? You told them you can't do that because . . . because I've been here so long, and I've worked so hard, and I know *Good Morning, New Jersey* like it's my own child. . . ." I mean, if it weren't for *Good Morning, New Jersey*, maybe I'd *have* my own child.

"His name is Chip," Oscar said.

Chip? *Chip?* They were giving my dream job away to some scrub named Chip?

21

"And he starts Monday."

I slumped, helpless against the onslaught.

"He has an MBA and a journalism degree from Columbia."

Wow. That was pretty good. I mean, nothing compared with three years at Fairleigh Dickinson and a frickin' *lifetime spent pouring out blood sweat and tears at this very studio*, but, hey. Pretty good. Had this supposedly fabulous Chip person ever been to New Jersey in his life? Had he interviewed Bon Jovi at the opening of the Prudential Center? Did someone with a name like Chip even know who Bon Jovi was?

"They're grooming him to run the whole station in a few years. I wish I could afford to keep you, Becky—but with your seniority . . ."

My insides felt hollowed out. I looked at Oscar in shock. He looked back at me, pitiful little undereducated me, with my stupid T-shirt and my stupid hopes and my stupid decade of living for this damn place. I couldn't stand being seen that way. I plunged my face into my hands.

"Shit," I mumbled against my palms. "Shit shit shit shit shit."

"Oh, Becky," Oscar said. "I'm so sorry. I fought them as hard as I could." He came back around his desk and put his hand on my arm. He probably meant it to be comforting, but it plopped there like a cold, dead fish.

"The only thing that makes this okay for me," he said, "is that I know you'll land on your feet."

Well, glad it's okay for *you*, I almost snapped, but for me it's a real bitch. But that would hardly have been professional. Hardly have been worthy of someone who was supposed to "land on her feet."

Ha! In this economy. With an education that apparently

wasn't even good enough to guarantee security at a job I've had since before I was legal.

"Me?" I managed to reply. "Of course. Yeah, definitely." Let me just go polish up my resume. I mean, *make* a resume. I mean, *learn* how to make a resume.

Shit.

3

stumbled into the hall, half blind with the tears I'd utterly failed to hold back. Fired. I'd been fired. Or laid off? Or . . . I didn't have a job. Either way.

It was dawn in New Jersey, and I didn't have a job.

Anna was waiting at my cubicle clad in a T-shirt that said WAY TO GO, BECKY! Well, at least she had that part right. I had a long, long way to go.

"What's going on?" she asked, the smile fading from her face as she got a good look at mine.

I filled her in on the details and watched her expression go from shock to outrage to bafflement. "What are you going to do?" she asked. The unspoken part of her question hung in the air: What are you going to do if not even this place will have you?

"I'm going to get a box," I replied. "And I'm going to empty out my desk. And you're going to help me."

She nodded, somber. "Right."

"But first"—I grimaced—"we're going to change our shirts."

After more than ten years at the station, I had a lot of stuff to load in the car, and I made everyone I found wearing one of those stupid WAY TO GO, BECKY! T-shirts help me pack up. Oscar was giving me six weeks' pay but had offered, *oh-so-generously*, to let me not do the six weeks of associated work, to give me time to find a new position.

A new position, away from Channel 9. The thought was inconceivable. Where would I be without this place? Who would I be? I'd been employed at Channel 9 since before Mom had sold her house and moved to the Sunshine State. I'd been at *Good Morning, New Jersey* since the year I'd lost my virginity. I'd been a production intern here when other folks my age were folding sweaters at the Gap. They probably wouldn't even hire me at the Gap because the only, only thing I'd ever known how to do was produce the morning news.

What in the world was I going to do now?

I tamped down my panic as Anna approached, then slapped on my bravest smile. She gave me a mock salute. "All packed up, chief."

"Great," I said. I took a deep breath. Here goes nothing.

"You're going to make it," she said. "I know you will."

I shrugged, like I hadn't even noticed that my entire professional life was a shambles. "You know what?" I said. "This is actually good news."

"Sure," Anna said, not entirely convinced.

"There are a lot of terrific opportunities out there."

"Absolutely," she agreed, though we both knew that was a load of bull.

I floundered. "Look at Chip. He got one."

"Uh . . . yeah," said Anna.

We stood in awkward silence for a moment.

"In fact," I said, trying my best to rally, "this is just what I needed. A little push from the nest. I've been here way too long."

"Right." Anna pumped her fist in the air, playing the supportive friend role as hard as she could.

I grabbed the very last box. "I need to take myself to the next level."

"Totally."

"Maybe to a network."

"Definitely."

"After all," I said, "it's only work. It's not my whole life, right?"

Anna opened her mouth to agree with me again, but this time, nothing came out.

The next morning, at 1:29 A.M., my eyes opened to darkness. I sat up pole-straight in bed and blinked until I could make out the details in my room. The shine of the TV screen on my dresser, the one on my bookshelf, the third on my storage chest. All dark and silent. I looked at the glowing numbers of my clock as it clicked over to 1:30. Nothing happened. No alarm. No music. No news to start the day. I had no reason to be awake. I had nothing to do.

I reached over and flipped on the light, then folded my hands in my lap. Nothing whatsoever to do.

My laptop lay on my bedside table. I'd been working on my resume the previous night before I went to bed. There really wasn't much in the way of content. One company, several titles, a smattering of local broadcasting awards. Oscar would give me an excellent reference, I knew. The trick would be translating that into opportunity.

I clicked through to my news bookmarks out of sheer habit, wondering if I should call Anna to make sure they were covering the minor earthquake rumbling through Nevada. But I was sure they would be. Plus, she'd probably berate me for not taking this opportunity to sleep in.

If there was a heaven, my dad was probably there shaking his head at me right now. I know Mom was, down in Florida. She hadn't said much when I'd left Fairleigh to take the assistant producer job all those years ago. After all, she'd never been to college, money was tight after my dad's death, and a bird in the hand was worth the two that might be in the bush when I and the other 150 FDU communication majors graduated with BAs. The way we both saw it, I was getting a jump on the competition. At least, that's what we'd thought back then. Apparently, a bigger jump could have been had if I'd had a trust fund and ten years to net myself an Ivy League MBA and a journalism degree. What was real-world experience compared with a string of letters after your name?

"Real-world experience." That wasn't all I'd dreamed television news was back then, watching the evening news with my dad. I'd seen Mike Pomeroy almost get blown to bits in Kosovo. I'd stared in rapture at the screen as he'd braved Hurricane Andrew to report in Florida. I'd listened as he'd interviewed Nelson Mandela days after his election in South Africa. And I knew that television news was where I belonged.

I clicked through to YouTube and typed "IBS evening news Nelson Mandela" into the search box. Forget C-SPAN and FOX News this morning. If I was going to get back in the game, I needed a little old-school inspiration.

. . .

Four weeks later, I was zero for forty on job applications. I'd started with the big guys, of course, though in retrospect, I probably should have waited on a few of those until I'd finessed my resume a bit. Or at least, that was the impression I'd gotten from the hiring manager at *Good Day, Tampa Bay*. After I'd taken her very helpful suggestions, I'd gotten written rejections from the next few places I'd tried.

Today, I was planning on following up with *Eyewitness News in Tulsa* and *Action News* in Pittsburgh. And if that didn't work, I was going to nail down the folks in Phoenix once and for all.

As soon as I was done at the Laundromat. Right now, my only clean shirt said I ACCEPT. Which was very much unacceptable attire, at least until I got a new job.

While waiting for my whites to brighten in the industrial washers, I started making calls. The results were rather less than heartening.

"... So if you hear of anything ... ," I said to one very apologetic HR staffer.

"Sure, Ms. Fuller. But you know, in this economy, and with the Internet ..."

"Or, you know, if anyone you know hears of anything ... ," I went on.

"Have you considered starting a blog?" asked the dude from the evening show in New Haven. "We just hired this really excellent blogger. Or vlogger. Or something. New media is totally the wave of the future."

"Is it now?" I asked wearily. I didn't think my laptop even had a webcam.

"Yeah." The guy lowered his voice. "In fact, I think I'm leaving for Gawker."

I wrote down Gawker on my list of possibilities. I was hip. I was with it. I could swing my smartphone with the best of them.

Not that people necessarily appreciated it when I did. Don't even get me started on my three rounds with *American Morning*. Oscar had used all his connections to get me a name to email my resume to, and then . . . I waited. And waited. And got tired of waiting, which is when I learned that not only do they not like smartphones at CNN, they don't like persistence, either.

Round One: "See," I explained, "on my BlackBerry it shows you opened the email, so I just wondered. Yeah, it shows . . . hello? Well, no, I didn't *hack your system!*"

Round Two: "Hi there, Becky Fuller again. Yes, I called yesterday, but I updated my resume last night"— this was after the hints from Tampa—"and I thought you might want the latest—oh, okay. Cool, I'll check with you some other time. How's tomorrow sound?"

Round Three: "When I called yesterday, your secretary was pretty sure you'd read the email. Yes, we resolved the whole issue with my BlackBerry notification. Well . . . oh. You filled the position? Oh. That's . . . terrific. Congratulations."

So much for moving south.

I bought books on finding jobs and tried to decipher metaphors about cheese and parachutes. I tried to adjust my circadian rhythms to a more diurnal schedule but gave up after two weeks of looking like a zombie and waking up at 1:30 A.M. no matter what I did. I reasoned with myself that it would be a waste of time anyway. As soon as I succeeded at resetting my internal clock, I'd get a new job and have to go back to my usual schedule. I thought a lot about a story I'd done two years ago on dealing with unemployment. I remembered the psychological expert talking about managing the fear and humiliation of being jobless during the job search, a time where you were supposed to project the most self-confidence.

I could not, unfortunately, recall any of her proposed solutions.

And then one afternoon, more than a month after my severance package with Channel 9 ran out, I was sitting on a park bench having my eighty-fifth pointless conversation with my eighty-fifth hiring manager. I'd exhausted every city with a broadcasting station in the United States and was probably paying roaming charges to chat with the polite and extremely apologetic employee of *Wake Up, Manitoba.*

"And by any chance do you think any other positions might be available soon?" I asked.

The guy laughed. "It's pretty much me and the cameraman up here."

"Who does your weather?" I asked.

"Local moose."

And just then, the call-waiting beeped. I checked the readout. A 212 number. Manhattan?

I quickly bid my adieus to the Canuck.

"Hello?" I asked cautiously.

"Is this Becky Fuller?" asked an unfamiliar voice. "This is Jerry Barnes, from IBS."

IBS? *The* IBS? I blinked, and my mouth opened and closed a few times, like a fish that can't figure out where all that nice, life-preserving water went and why there's a hook in its gills.

"Yes," I croaked. "This is Becky." Had I sent my resume to any HR manager named Jerry Barnes?

"I'm an old friend of Oscar's," said Jerry. "We worked together in the early days, and he passed your name along to me. . . ."

God bless Oscar! So he *had* been looking out for me.

"Anyway," said Jerry. "I've got this opening at my morning show—"

An IBS morning show? Awesome. "Tell me more!"

"Well," Jerry warned, "I feel I should tell you, it's a really tough gig—"

"I like tough."

"So Oscar told me," said Jerry. "When are you available for an interview?"

I somehow resisted saying that now worked just fine.

4

There I was, standing before the imposing doors of the famous IBS building. You could have the totally over-exposed 30 Rock, you could have the CBS building, Eero Saarinen design and all. Maybe they had more history, more gravitas. But they didn't dominate the skyline. This glass monolith on Bryant Park was all I needed to be happy.

As long as they gave me the job.

I checked my reflection one last time in the glass door. No lipstick on my teeth, auburn hair still neat and sleek in its chignon. I'd trimmed my bangs this morning—a dangerous prospect, I know, but they'd turned out great. Maybe that was a good omen. Black suit. Power pumps. My mother's tiny diamond drop pendant for luck . . . I was ready.

After receiving my guest pass, I was ushered by an assistant into the sleek and very cold office of Jerry Barnes, this old friend of Oscar's who—judging from the square footage in this room alone—had clearly done much better in life than my former boss. Jerry was tall and fit, with network exec hair and a network exec suit, set off by a surprisingly un-network-exec-like pair of brown, horn-rimmed glasses. After dispensing with the formalities, he scanned my resume as if he hadn't already seen it, and gestured for me to sit down across from him.

"Oscar says you're very talented and you work incredibly hard," said Jerry, as if he didn't quite believe it. "Says you're the most promising producer he's ever fired."

"Well, that's good," I said. "I think." Because what did that say, really? That I was good—but not as good as the other senior producer he'd hired?

"So," he asked, as if it was the most casual question in the world, "you're a fan of our morning show?"

I smiled broadly and lied my ass off. "It has many interesting—"

"Yeah, we know. It's terrible." Jerry waved a hand at me. No bullshit here. "You know morning news shows are usually the cash cows. The foreign bureaus? The breaking coverage? All the political convention crap? Morning news pays for all of that. Evening news looks down on daytime programming, but it foots their bills."

"Great," I said in what I prayed was a simultaneously sage and supportive tone.

"Except," said Jerry, "for our network."

"Ah."

"Our show is perpetually in fourth place behind the *Today* show, *Good Morning America,* and that thing on CBS, whatever it's called."

Yeah, no one watched that show either.

Jerry sighed. "The anchors of our show are difficult and semi-talented—"

I pursed my lips and shook my head. "Colleen Peck is a pro—"

"Hei—nous!" Jerry snapped.

Well, at least she didn't fall asleep in the middle of the broadcast. "Paul McVee," I said. "Fine reporter."

Jerry shot me an incredulous look. "He's foul."

"Look, Mr. Barnes," I said.

"Jerry."

"Jerry, I—"

But he wasn't finished. "*Daybreak*'s facilities are antiquated, it's understaffed and underfunded, any executive producer who works there will be publicly ridiculed and overworked, and, oh, the pay is awful."

I raised my eyebrows. "How awful?"

"About half of what you were making over there at *Hey, How the Hell Are You, New Jersey*."

"*Good Morning, New Jersey*," I corrected.

"Whatever." He waved at me again. "I've offered this job to twenty-two people already and they've all turned me down."

Twenty-two. I swallowed. Really? I wondered how many of those twenty-two were being headhunted away from current jobs, and how many were, like me, unemployed. How many people did he want for this position more than he did me? People who might be out there snatching up any other available job?

"Yes," I said bravely. "But I—"

"Frankly," Jerry admitted, "if I could find someone who was qualified, you wouldn't be sitting in that chair."

I reeled back in that chair as if I'd been slapped.

He counted off my disqualifications. "You've never been an executive producer, you're too young, no one's ever heard of you, and your education?" He shot me a look of disdain. "Three—not four—years at Fairleigh Ridiculous?"

"Dickin—"

"Did I miss anything?" He folded his arms.

I cleared my throat. "No."

"Okay, Becky Fuller," he said. "So. Speak."

"Okay." I took a deep breath. This might be my only chance. "Is *Daybreak* a shitty show? Yes. But it's on a network, and not just any network—this is one of the most legendary news divisions in the history of television."

Jerry gave me goggle eyes.

"All this show needs," I continued, my tone turning passionate, "is someone who believes in it, who understands that a national platform is an invaluable resource, that no story is too low and no story is too high to reach for." I stopped, a little breathless.

"Are you going to sing now?" Jerry asked.

"*Daybreak* needs exactly what I need," I cried. "Someone who believes it can succeed. Trust me, I know there's no reason you should believe in me except that I work harder than anyone else. First in. Last out. I know a shitload more about the news than someone whose daddy paid for them to smoke bongs and take semiotics at Harvard."

For once, Jerry had gone quiet. Oh, crap. I checked above Jerry's desk for any sign of a diploma. Please tell me he didn't go to Harvard.

"And I devote myself *completely* to my job," I said quickly, while the Harvard crack lingered. "It's all I do. It's all I am. You can ask anyone."

"Well, that's . . ." Jerry grimaced. ". . . Embarrassing."

"It is," I agreed. "It's also true." Dear God, was it true. And for the past two months, the daily five hours between my waking up and the advent of dawn I'd spent doing absolutely nothing had totally driven home that fact. I needed the news far, far more than I'd needed anything. Except coffee. Or maybe a boyfriend.

Actually, God, if I get this job, I promise I'll stop complaining about the boyfriend.

He studied me for a moment, arms folded, the horn-rimmed glasses the only thing keeping his gaze from turning skanky. I stared back, chin lifted. I was dead serious about what I'd said. And this was so obviously my only shot.

Finally, he said, "I'll let you know."

"Okay," I said, and rose. I began backing out the door. "I'll just . . . show myself out, then. When do you think—"

"I'll let you know," he repeated, and turned back to his work.

"Do you have . . . All my info's on the resume." Oh God, I hoped I was backing out the actual door. I risked a look behind me. Yep. Door. "Okay!" I said. "Bye! Thanks for . . . thanks."

"Uh-huh." He didn't look up. Was that a bad sign? Did I screw up? Sound too eager? Too desperate? Too oddly obsessed with the very idea of morning news shows?

I walked to the elevator in a daze, going over every nuance in Jerry's expression post–impassioned speech. Was he impressed? Disgusted? Scared? Had I screwed up my only chance? The door opened and I stepped in. Should I have reminded him about how I was applicant number *twenty-three*—acted, like the applicants before me, like I was too good for *Daybreak*?

A man stepped into the elevator beside me. About my age, with six inches on me—even in my heels—and absurdly handsome, with good hair, chiseled features, and an untucked dress shirt of matching quality. At the very least, he hadn't just flubbed a major job interview. He looked from me to the elevator control panel and then back to me.

"It's these buttons right here," he said.

"Oh." I snapped out of it. "Um, lobby, please."

He pressed the button. "Good day so far?"

"Don't think so," I said, too rattled to be anything but candid. "Talked too much. Ruined it."

"Making up for it now?" he said, mocking my tone.

The elevators doors started to close when a hand slid in and stopped them. The doors reopened, and in walked Mike Pomeroy.

I gasped. Ohmigod. Mike Pomeroy. *Mike Pomeroy!* A little older, perhaps, than when I used to idolize him on the nightly news, but still impressive, with silver hair and a rugged face and intelligent eyes and *oh wow, oh wow, Mike Pomeroy is standing in the elevator with me right now.*

Mike Pomeroy gave a perfunctory nod to the cute guy as the elevator began its descent. I opened my mouth to speak, then bit my tongue. I tried to stare at the floor numbers on the monitor, but *MikePomeroyisstandingnextome he'sbreathingmyair MikePomeroyohmigod.*

"Sir," I said, turning to face him. I couldn't help myself. "I . . . wow. I am . . . such an admirer, sir. I . . . Just wow."

The other man looked amused by my outburst.

"Big, *big* fan. Big. Huge. We watched you growing up . . . my whole family did. Of all the anchors I ever saw, you were by far the best reporter. I mean it. When you were in Kosovo, *I* was in Kosovo. You know? Wow."

Mike Pomeroy looked at the other guy. "She work for you?"

"No," he said. "I'm just here to teach her how to use the elevator."

The door opened at my back. Mike turned back to me. "You done?"

"Yes," I said. Wow, *Mike Pomeroy was addressing me.* "Sorry. Yes."

He gestured past me, to the exit. "May I?"

"Oh." I scooted out of the way. "Yes. Sure. Of course. Sorry."

Mike Pomeroy left. As the doors closed, I sighed. "Oh my God, I can't believe I just . . . do you know him?"

The elevator dinged again and the doors opened. "Yes," said the man, his face and tone equally stiff. "He's the third-worst person in the world." Then he got off.

I struggled to collect myself all the way down to the lobby.

Well, I suppose my visit to IBS wasn't a total waste of time. After all, I'd been face-to-face with Mike Pomeroy. Probably made an even bigger fool of myself to him than I had to Jerry Barnes, but still. It had been worth it. Mike Pomeroy!

Guess that was my first and last chance to be in an elevator with him, though. I trudged across the IBS plaza, no longer caring if I scuffed the toes of my power pumps. I pulled off my IBS guest badge and tossed it in the nearest trash can. The pedestrian traffic flowed around me, busy New Yorkers, with jobs, livelihoods, boyfriends. Reasons for existing.

My BlackBerry started buzzing in my pocket. I pulled it out and checked the number.

IBS.

I answered, heedless of the city noise and the sound of the fountain in the plaza and the fact that it was not super-professional to shout "Hello!" into a phone.

"Okay," said Jerry. "Let's do it."

"Really?" I cried.

"I told you it didn't pay much though, right?"

He had indeed. Less even than my old job, and I'd have to relocate to Manhattan. Still, right now I was being paid nothing *and* I wasn't working in television. So it was still a step up.

"I'll take it."

"Be here Monday." He hung up.

For a moment I was utterly still, a high heel–clad rock in the river of Manhattan foot traffic. And then I leapt for joy. I started whooping and screaming, scaring at least ten pedestrians. I twirled around a few times for good measure, then danced down the street toward the nearest entrance to the subway.

Becky Fuller, Executive Producer of IBS's *Daybreak*.

I'd done it.

I was already trolling craigslist for apartments on the ferry ride back to Jersey.

"No, I don't have any pets," I explained to the dude with the promising-sounding studio. "Loud parties?" I laughed. "Not unless you think me and some raw cookie dough is a party. And I don't mind the lack of a view. I actually find looking at a wall kind of soothing."

"Lady," he said, "you sound weird, but you can come take a look."

The apartment wasn't about to win any design awards, but it would do. I devoted the rest of the week to making my move. I reserved a U-Haul on my BlackBerry after signing the lease, and picked up some boxes from the packing place near my house on the way home. Sadly, I only needed three, though at least it meant saving on storage fees. My new place was *tiny*. I could brush my teeth, make toast, pick out clothes, open the window, and see who was at the front door, all without moving my feet. I guess that's what you got when you wanted to live in Manhattan. But if it meant my own morning show, I'd live in a footlocker.

Packing my furniture didn't take too long either. IKEA stuff, as it turns out, is as easy to dismantle as it is to put together. Except for the futon. That college-era monstrosity was so ready for the curb. Within a few days, I had a new apartment and a new sofa, and was all set for my new life.

Maybe this time, I'd actually have a life.

Anna flipped when I told her, over drinks my last night in Jersey. Well, my last afternoon, as we were both committed to morning show schedules.

"*Daybreak?*" she said. "I didn't even know that show was still on."

I had a feeling I was going to get that a lot. "Well, you will soon. Now that I'm in charge."

Anna clinked her glass against mine. "Here's to that!"

I also told her about meeting Mike Pomeroy, and my unfortunate case of verbal diarrhea.

"Yikes," said Anna. "What has he been up to recently? I don't think I've seen him on *The Nightly News* lately."

"He got fired," I said. "Something about calling some politician a shithead or a used tampon; I can't remember the details. But it was on air. The fines alone—"

"Then what was he doing in the building?" she asked.

"He still does the occasional story," I explained. "Just isn't anchoring anymore. I bet he's still under contract there."

Anna shot me a look. "Becky," she warned. "Do not stalk Mike Pomeroy."

"I won't."

"Seriously. I hear he carries a gun."

"I won't!" I insisted.

Much.

And then, before I knew it, it was my first day at IBS. I put on my best suit, dragged out the heels again, and went to town with the straightening iron. My first day as an executive producer, and I wanted to look the part. Besides, like Jerry said, a lot of people there were already expecting me to fail. I could not afford to look like anything but an absolute ballbreaker.

I was from New Jersey. We know how to break balls there.

Inside the atrium, I waited for my escort to take me to my new office. My brand-new briefcase rested by my side, looking neat and professional and executive. I straightened my skirt and took a deep breath and waited.

The monitor in the lobby was playing *Daybreak*. I could see Paul McVee and Colleen Peck, the two anchors, bantering on the show's signature sunshine-colored set.

"Tomorrow," Colleen was saying brightly but vapidly, like the ex–beauty queen she was, "we'll show you what to do with all those shampoo bottles you've got lying around with only an inch of shampoo left in the bottom." She looked at Paul and smiled. "I've always wondered what to do about that."

"Oh, I know," Paul replied. "That is a toughie."

Someone passing in front of the monitor looked at the screen, then rolled his eyes.

I straightened in my seat. Okay, I clearly had my work cut out for me—no argument there. I needed to improve not only the show, but its reputation, even internally at IBS.

"Also," said Paul, "we'll have more on the flooding in Iowa. Finally, some better weather news on the way for those folks."

I raised my eyebrows. Better than *flooding*? Really? Apparently the bar for improving this show wasn't set too high.

Colleen broke in. "So please join us tomorrow and"— she paused dramatically for her sign-off—"thank you for spending your morning here at *Daybreak*."

"Take care, everyone!" Paul said with a wave at the audience.

Colleen nodded like a queen issuing a last-minute pardon. Which, given the quality of the show, wasn't too far off. "*Goodbye*."

I sighed.

The guard behind the desk looked at me. "You interviewing at *Daybreak*? Assistant? Intern?"

I patted my hair. "Actually, um, I'm the new executive producer over there."

"Another one?" the guard scoffed.

"Excuse me?"

The guard lifted his hands in surrender. "Just saying. Don't unpack."

Great. Even the security guard thought I couldn't hack it. Maybe the straightening iron hadn't worked as well as I'd hoped.

Just then, I saw a man walking toward me. "Becky Fuller?" He extended his hand.

I popped up and accepted it. "That's me."

He gave me a weak smile. "I'm Lenny Bergman."

"Associate producer," we said at the same time.

"Yes," I went on. "I know who you are. You started out at WABC, then two years at CBS, been here thirteen years."

"That's right," he said, impressed. Lenny was in his forties, a bit portly, with hair in need of a cut and a carriage like he bore the weight of the world on his shoulders. Was this what it was to work at *Daybreak* for thirteen years? This constant look of defeat?

"My only question is, why didn't they bump you up?"

"Not for me," he said.

I shook my head. He didn't want a promotion?

Catching my disbelief, he shrugged. "I did it for a couple of weeks once, then they put me back at number two."

"Why?"

"Apparently, the crying was distracting."

Oh. I forced myself to nod, as if I understood.

"But you'll love it," he said as quickly as possible. "It's a *great* job."

The security guard snorted.

5

After the requisite stop at HR to fill out all my paperwork and pick up my ID badge, Lenny led me into the bowels of the IBS building. Our first step was a long, long trip down a surprisingly rickety elevator for such a new building. Next, we traversed a series of increasingly shabby and narrow hallways while Lenny filled me in on the schedule.

"Our morning meeting is at five A.M.," he explained to me.

"Isn't that a little late?" I asked. Even at Channel 9, we had more than a two-hour window for last-minute adjustments.

We flattened ourselves against the wall as a bunch of tech folks passed, toting cables and props. The hallway went on, tunneling its way to what might as well have been the center of the earth. Here and there lay disused pieces of office furniture. I twisted and turned to avoid bashing into things as I tried to keep pace with Lenny, who clearly knew this rabbit warren like the back of his hand.

"It's just that," I said, as he sidestepped a dead potted ficus, "I'm used to early hours. . . ."

"Hmm," said Lenny, as if the thought had never occurred to him. "Maybe we need better donuts." He started pointing places out as we drew closer and closer to the control room—break room this way, ladies' room down that corridor—but I couldn't get past the schedule.

"At the *Today* show," I said, "the senior staff is in by four thirty."

Lenny stopped and turned around, an amused expression on his face. "Yeah. We're just like the *Today* show," he said, his tone facetious. "Without the money, viewers, respect . . . but, you know, kinda similar."

And with that, he opened the door marked "Control Room," and led me into the interior of an abandoned Cold War submarine.

Well, not really. But if Lenny had told me that this was the set for some IBS movie-of-the-week version of *The Hunt for Red October*, I wouldn't have been surprised.

"Is there . . . electricity in here?" I asked with horror.

"Sometimes the line monitor turns off and I have to kick it while holding on to a coat hanger."

"Ah." Guess I had my answer.

Lenny watched me take it all in. "So, Jerry give you any money to upgrade the control room or the studio?"

"He told me he's cutting the budget twenty percent."

"Damn," said Lenny. "I had my heart set on a new coat hanger."

I laughed. Lenny I liked, as long as he could keep from crying.

He shrugged. "Suppose that's what I get for working at a network with the same acronym as irritable bowel syndrome."

"Bowel" was right. I looked around at the ridiculously out-moded control room. And I'd thought things at Channel 9 needed an upgrade. But still, it was a control room, and I hadn't been in one of those for quite a while. I took a deep breath. Ah, I love the smell of napalm in the morning.

"Look," I said to Lenny. "I'm not an idiot. I know what this show is up against. But just because no one watches it and it has sucked mightily in the past doesn't mean it needs to suck any longer. I won't let it. It's a privilege to work on a network show and *I* for one am not going to let that opportunity go by."

Lenny gaped at me. "Are you going to sing now?"

I grinned. If that's what it took to wake these people up. "So, what do you say? Are we going to give this thing a shot?"

"If you insist," Lenny said with a smile.

"Great." I pushed at the sleeves of my blazer. "Let's have at it." I strode to the door and pulled the doorknob.

It came off in my hand.

"That was one of our best doorknobs," said Lenny.

Lenny continued the tour, leading me past Craft Services and toward the dressing room. The walls were covered with shots of *Daybreak* cohosts through the years. I noted without surprise that though the fashions changed, their faces and hair never did. Colleen Peck had sported an unaging, cheerful smile and a Martha Stewartesque blond coif since the mid-nineties. Paul McVee was her visual opposite: dark hair, a rare smile—good thing too, since it could sometimes come across as a bit too Anthony Perkins—and rather more hair product than any one man could possibly need.

"Colleen has been here forever," Lenny was saying. "Don't mention that, by the way. But McVee is paid more—don't mention that, either."

"Right," I said, and snagged a bagel from a Craft Services table. I was actually surprised to hear it. Though I supposed they had as much trouble wooing hosts to the show as they did producers. Maybe McVee viewed it as hazard pay.

"They hate each other—don't mention that—but that's because Colleen actually hates everyone—don't mention that—and she used to sleep with Paul, who threw her over for her own assistant—don't—"

"—Mention that," I said. "Got it."

"And make sure after you talk to Colleen, you come get me *before* you talk to McVee. So I can go with you."

I furrowed my brow. "Why?"

"Just . . . trust me, okay?" Lenny paused outside Colleen's dressing room. "You ready?"

I nodded and knocked.

"Enter." Colleen's voice was almost unrecognizable as she issued the command. I gave Lenny a look, and his expression said it all.

Don't say I didn't warn you.

As it turned out, no warning from Lenny would have sufficed to prepare me for the amount of hostility Colleen aimed at me from the second I walked through her door. Gone was her on-air persona, full of smiles and soft-spoken bonhomie. The Colleen Peck I met was a rabid tiger—eyes flashing, hair tossing, mouth twisted into a snarl. She didn't even let me introduce myself before she started ranting.

"Do you know how many EPs I have had in the last eleven years? *Fourteen.*" She stepped out of her heels and shoved her feet into a pair of fuzzy slippers. "If they're stupid, they get fired, and if they're smart, they quit. And now"—she gave me the most contemptuous up-down I've ever received—"now look what I've got."

I stuck out my hand. "Hi, I'm Becky."

"Becky." She glared at my hand, but didn't touch it. "Are you stupid or smart?"

"I'm going with smart," I said. "And staying."

Colleen gave a rather inelegant snort and turned to her dressing table. "Do you think I like being in last place?" she asked as she smeared moisturizer on her face. "Think it's fun to work for a network that spends more on one episode of a dating show about a bachelor dwarf than on our entire weekly budget?"

Was that true? Granted, *A Little Bit o' Love* was a surprisingly entertaining program, but still.

"The only reason I haven't been fired," she said, whirling on me, "is that I'm cheap and I have a high Q rating with bored, postmenopausal women who buy the advertisers' junk."

She poked her perfectly manicured nail at me until I backed up a few steps. "I've never had a decent coanchor, just a revolving door of cretinous morons. Our ratings are in the crapper. How long can the show limp along this way?" She spun and disappeared into her closet.

I peered after her, but she slammed the door in my face. I wasn't entirely sure whether or not she was looking for a real answer to her question. And it was a good question, too. The show couldn't go on like this. And I had no intention of letting it. "Look, Colleen," I said to the slats of the door. "I know the history of the show. I know everyone has been through a lot and—"

Colleen whipped the door open and stepped out, clad in pants and a fitted T-shirt and looking every bit as impeccable as she did in her stage clothes. That she'd been able to pull it off standing in a dark, cramped closet was nothing short of a miracle.

A very intimidating, possibly sorcery-related miracle.

"You," Colleen stated in a haughty tone, "will fail. Like everyone else. And then you will be gone. Like everyone else." She advanced again, and again I retreated. Some ball-breaker, me. "And I will still me here, pulling this train up the hill with my teeth."

Her very white, very even, and likely very sharp teeth. The ones she was currently baring in my direction. I realized I'd underestimated this one. The pageant queen air she adopted in front of the cameras hid the piranha underneath.

I wondered if I could work with that. Rebrand her as a tough, no-nonsense kind of broad. Bette Davis. Katharine Hepburn. Barbara Stanwyck. People liked that.

She poked at me again. "You think it's fun to get your ass kicked?"

I stumbled back until I was right on the threshold. Though, of course, people really only liked tough broads when their ire was directed elsewhere, as Colleen was so very helpfully illustrating for me. "Well, I—"

"Welcome to *Daybreak*—Gidget," said Colleen. And she shut the door in my face.

"Okay," I said to the door. "Good talk! Terrific feedback. Looking forward to . . ." I trailed off. "Okay then."

Right. Well, Colleen would be a bit prickly, but I was sure we could learn to work together. After all, she seemed committed to the same cause as me: *Daybreak*. We could . . . pull that train up the hill by our teeth together. Or something.

As I turned, I spotted Paul McVee heading down the corridor.

"Paul!" I shouted.

He turned, and I got the full effect of his—er—enhancements. Without the help of the camera, they were a bit . . . valley of the uncanny. If I'd run into him outside Madame Tussauds, I might have mistaken him for his own figurine. His skin was too tan, his teeth were too shiny, and his hair was too shellacked. But I pasted on a smile every bit as fake as the cleft in his chin and walked briskly up to him.

"Becky Fuller," I said. "I'll be your new executive producer. So thrilled to meet you. I—"

He kept walking toward his dressing room, ignoring the hand I held out for him to shake and eschewing any kind of greeting, even the one Colleen had made me suffer through.

"When you get a chance," I called after him, as if he were paying the slightest bit of attention, "I'd love to talk to you about some ideas. I'd like to move something around in the budget, see if we can get you on the street doing more remotes—"

He stopped at his door. "Yeahhh," he said slowly. "I don't like to leave the studio. I like . . . climate control."

Right—otherwise he'd melt. I caught up to him, determined to salvage the introduction. "Oh, I see. Well, I'm sure you have plenty of ideas for other—"

He shrugged. "Not really. I punch in, I punch out. No complaints here."

Oh-kaay. "See, because Colleen and I were just tossing around some possible—"

"Of course," he continued, swinging open the door to his dressing room, "I'd always be happy to discuss this matter *privately*." He waggled his plucked eyebrows at me.

"Uh . . ." Okay, maybe I was just reading it wrong. After

all, I'd spoken to Colleen in her dressing room. Such as it was. I peered inside. Hold on—was that a *cot*?

He looked down at my feet. "What size do you wear? Six and a half? Seven?"

"Seven and a half narrow," I replied, confused.

"Uh-huh." He cocked his head, still staring at my heels. "How do you feel about having your feet photographed?"

Lenny came rushing down the hall. "Becky, Paul, *there* you are." He gave me a look that said *I told you so*.

I gave him one back that I hoped communicated the finest in New Jersian: *I don't give a shit*.

This was *my* show now.

The next gauntlet was my first staff meeting. The employees convened in *Daybreak*'s conference room, which unfortunately was every bit as shabby as the rest of the studio. But at the same time, I was impressed. The staff—*my* staff—was about four times larger than what we'd had at Channel 9. At least fifteen people ringed the table before me, and every last one of them was trying to size me up.

I wore my cool, calm, and collected expression like battle armor, and took a seat next to Lenny. "We all here?" I asked.

Colleen rolled her eyes, exasperated. "Missing McVee," she said. "Shocker."

Lenny jumped in, "McVee doesn't always come to these."

The hell he doesn't. "Punch in, punch out" was now permanently off the plate for my anchors. I turned to one of the interns sitting behind me and gave her a sweet smile. "Tell Paul we need him, please." And if he dared to make some kind of pervy crack about her shoes, I'd have his head.

"Okay then," I said. "Hi, guys. I'm Becky Fuller. So . . ." I tapped the edge of my folder against the table. "Let's just dive in."

And dive in they did. For the next few minutes, it seemed like I was being besieged from all sides by story ideas, scheduling crises, inane queries, and every bit of demographical indecision known to mankind.

"Tomorrow, Rocco di Spirito wants to make lasagna," said one producer.

"Great," I said.

"I told him we did that last week with the Barefoot Contessa, but he's insisting. What do I do?"

Oh. Not so great.

Lisa, whom I recognized as the entertainment reporter, piped up, "For next week, I want to do a piece on juice cleanses—all the celebs are doing them and they have amazing powers of rejuvenization."

"Rejuv—"

"My idea," she barreled on, "is that I get a juice cleanse and then we can, like, measure my toxins."

Her *toxins*?

"For the psychic pet interview," another producer asked, "the living room set or on stools? And do you want a parakeet or an iguana?"

"ABC says we can't have Eva Longoria until three weeks after *Good Morning America* gets her. What do we do?" asked a third.

A fourth spoke up. "You think you've got problems? They're only offering us the third lead of the Patrick Dempsey movie. Do we even want him?"

"Look," said a fifth, fed up with the trials of dealing with celebs and their demands. "I've got a *real* story. A great story out of Tampa about a retirement account scam. Great victims, great visuals, but we've gotta move quick, since they're dropping like flies. Should we send a team or use local talent?"

"A team!" said a sixth producer. "When the sound mixer in the control room is on the fritz again? It's going to cost at least ten grand to fix it, and I have no idea where we're supposed to get that money, unless it's from the news budget."

At this point, Ernie Appleby, the *Daybreak* weatherman, pulled two giant metal weather vanes out from under the table. One was topped with a rooster, the other with a horse. "I'd like to do a feature on weather vanes. They are fascinating. Like, did you know the word 'vane' is from the Old English 'fana,' which means 'weathercock'?"

That shut everyone up for a moment. Except for the fourth producer, who snickered. We were all frozen by the sight of Ernie's weathercocks.

And then another producer meekly raised her hand. "For that piece on baby food," she asked, "do you want an actual baby? And if so: White? Black? Hispanic? Asian? Brown-haired, blond-haired? Teeth? No teeth?"

They all stared at me, expecting answers. And as the silence stretched on, Colleen rolled her eyes at Lenny. Paul McVee chose that moment to make his entrance.

He leaned casually against the door frame. "Ah, here we all are, getting together to figure out how to go about making the worst show on television even more pathetic. *That* I certainly wouldn't want to miss." He glared down his nose at me and said in a voice of pure derision, "Now, what do *you* want?"

They all looked at Paul, then back to me. They all thought I was a loser, from Paul and Colleen all the way down to the intern taking notes at my back.

They hadn't seen anything yet.

I took a deep breath and turned to the first producer. "Tell Rocco," I said, "that if he insists on lasagna, he'll be bumped."

I focused on Lisa. " 'Toxins' can't be 'measured.' And the word is *'rejuvenation.'* "

I swiveled to face the second producer. "Living room. Parakeet."

To the third: "Tell Longoria's people she can't plug her next movie unless we get her within a week of GMA."

To the fourth: "I don't want the third lead, I want Dempsey. Tell *his* people if they'll do it we'll run him in the first hour and let him talk about recycling or endangered falcons or whatever it is his thing is."

"Ernie," I said to the weatherman. *"Weather vanes?* Are you kidding me? Come on."

"The Tampa story sounds great," I said to the fifth, "but we're going to have to use local talent. Because"—I looked at the sixth—"we have to get that sound board fixed. Look for the ten grand in the budget. I noticed the hair and makeup number is way too high." I glanced at Colleen. "You can share your hair person with Lisa on her days."

Colleen gasped, horrified by the notion.

I tapped my pen against my chin. "Let's see, did I forget anything? Right. Asian baby, no teeth. And let's do lesbian parents if we can."

The producer jotted that down. Everyone who wasn't writing furiously was staring at me, mouth agape. But I wasn't done yet. Not by a long shot.

I nodded to Paul McVee. "Oh, and Paul? *You're fired.*"

6

Paul began sputtering.

"FI-RED," I repeated. Out of the corner of my eye, I saw something unexpected flash across Colleen's face. Shock, yes, but also . . . was that respect? Or was I just misreading her ability to work around the Botox?

I picked up my coffee cup and took a sip as the ex-anchor of IBS's *Daybreak* exited stage left. I heard the door shut—slam, actually. I heard a whole lot of deafening silence as every other employee of *Daybreak* sat in utter astonishment. And then, even more astonishing, I heard someone start to clap. And then a few more people joined in.

I gave Lenny a tiny, smug smile over the rim of my mug, and hoped no one noticed that the knuckles on my hand had gone corpse-white.

We tried to continue the meeting after that, but a funny thing happened—no one had any more questions. Eventually,

I gave up and dismissed them, and everyone practically bolted from the room. After all, there were emails to send and phone calls to make and the juiciest bit of gossip IBS had seen in months to share: The new executive producer of *Daybreak* had fired the anchor on her very first day.

Had I heard the news, I might not have believed it myself.

Even Colleen vanished, possibly to contact her agent and get him to double-check her contract. Colleen didn't worry me, though. She was prickly, but she was solid—possibly the only solid aspect of the entire show.

And now I'd scared the entire staff into realizing this.

"Well," said Lenny, once we were alone.

"Well," I said, and took another sip. I was going to run out of coffee soon, and then what would I do with my hands? I was pretty sure they would shake if they weren't gripping the mug so hard.

"Well, I guess I should see about that new sound mixer," Lenny said.

"You do that." I finally relinquished my stranglehold on the mug, but then immediately started flipping through the nearest folder.

"What . . ." He hesitated. "What are . . . um . . . you going to do?"

"Oh, I don't know," I said. "Maybe go have a chat with Jerry Barnes?"

"That sounds like a good idea," said Lenny. "Considering."

"Yeah," I agreed. "Considering."

Jerry's assistant had already heard by the time I got up there. Little wonder, given the labyrinth I had to traverse to escape from the *Daybreak* set.

"He wants to see you," she told me. "But he's out right now."

"Oh," I said. So Jerry had heard too. "Should I come back later?"

She shot me a look. "No, it means you should go find him." She lifted her phone receiver. "Want me to get you his present coordinates?"

Thanks to the assistant, I was able to intercept Jerry at the corner of Fifty-ninth Street and Fifth Avenue. He was checking out the display at the Apple store when I caught up to him.

"You," he said, looking at a waterfall of candy-colored iPods.

"Hi."

"Congratulations. You broke *Daybreak*." Still no eye contact. Was that how things worked here at IBS?

"Well, now, Jerry—," I began.

"First day and you flushed your anchor, with no money to pay for another one."

"He was lowering the morale of the show," I argued.

Now he turned to me. "Is that even possible?"

I stood my ground. It was possible *now*. I had morale, and damn it, I was going to make sure everyone else did too, if I had to shove it down their throats. Or up other orifices.

"You must have people under contract," I said. "Local anchors. Reporters. I'll find one. Promote from within. It will be good for people on the show to see that."

Jerry didn't look convinced. "Go nuts," he said. "Find someone great. Just can't cost me a penny."

He turned and started down the street. I called after him. "What if I give them one of my three pennies?"

"That's enough pluck out of you," he called back.

Oh no it wasn't. If I was going to find a new anchor—and not just any anchor, but one who would help me revitalize the show—I was going to have to find a whole new vein of Fuller pluck to mine. I was going to have to gird my loins, roll up my sleeves, put my nose to the grindstone, and engage in other metaphorical hardworking activities—and quickly, or *Daybreak* would indeed end up even more broken than before.

As soon as I got back to the office, I pulled the audition tapes of every newsman IBS had under contract with even a modicum of screen time. There had to be someone promising in here. Some plucky, personable newscaster just aching for a little bit of national exposure. Someone like me, who'd maybe been overlooked before because they didn't have the proper pedigree, but was chafing at the bit to show what they could do. And I'd pull them from obscurity and show them off to the world.

Hey, a girl could dream.

At least, she could dream for the first forty-three audition tapes. After that, things got a little hairy. Or toothy, in the case of the latest candidate, who appeared to have borrowed the mandibles of a horse for this broadcast.

"It was another nail-biter on Wall Street today . . ."

"And he'd know from biting," Lenny grumbled. He was seated by my side and was no more enthused by this process than I was.

". . . As the Dow rose eighty points, only to plunge two hundred points right before closing."

"He's not that bad," I said.

"Sure," replied Lenny. "Put a saddle on him and he's good to go."

I clicked off horse face and began rifling through our remaining DVDs. "Okay, who's next?"

Lenny stretched and rose. "Sorry. Gotta get home and see

the wife and kids." He looked down at me, still studying the pile of tapes. "You have kids?"

"What?" I asked. "No."

"Husband?" he tried. "Boyfriend?"

"Me?" I said. "What? No, no."

He laughed. "Oh, I'm sorry. What a stupid question. Of course, because you're hideous and repulsive."

I shook my head. "Damn it, where did I put that Miami DVD?"

"Or something like that," he added, then grabbed his jacket.

I waved him off. Even if I did have a boyfriend, or a husband, or kids, they couldn't begrudge my staying late on my first day at my own television show. Especially given that if I didn't find a solution to the problem I'd caused this morning, I might sink the show for good.

Eventually, however, the rest of the staff left me alone in the twisted passageways of the studio, and as the rooms went dark and still around me, I began to wonder what the screens in my office had to offer that my laptop in my apartment didn't. So Chinese takeout and pajamas it was. I boxed up the rest of the audition tapes and headed out.

I hit the lobby, balancing files, my briefcase, and the box of DVD jewel cases. My friend the security guard had also left for the night. But I wasn't entirely alone.

"Hey there," said a voice. "If it isn't Mike Pomeroy's Number One Fan."

I turned. The handsome young man from the elevator was coming through the front door, a bag of takeout in his hands. "Oh, God, that was embarrassing. I can't believe you saw that. I may have to have you killed."

He raised his eyebrows.

"I'm Becky Fuller," I said.

"Wait a second." The guy held out his hand. "The EP who took out McVee? You're a legend already. I believe you *might* have me killed if I step out of line. I'm Adam Bennett. I'm a producer upstairs at *7 Days*. . . ."

I shook his hand.

"So," he went on, "word's out you're looking for a new anchor." He checked out the DVDs at the top of my pile. "Oh, no, this guy? You can't use him. He's practically Mr. Ed."

"He's not so bad," I said, but I couldn't convince even myself. "I mean, as long as we remember to keep our hand flat when we feed him a carrot."

Adam laughed. "You always work this late, or you moonlighting at an evening program?"

"No," I said. "Well, sometimes I stay this late. Yes. Basically yes. Pretty much."

He laughed again, then held the door open for me. "Good luck, Becky Fuller."

"Thanks, Adam Bennett." I went through the door, then stopped on the street for a moment and watched him through the glass. Another untucked dress shirt, his hair mussed by the wind on the plaza. Cute guy. Bet he knew it, too. Bet no one ever gave him lip at a staff meeting. Bet his dating life put mine to shame.

Shake it off, Becky. I knew I'd better head home. I had a long night ahead of me.

Back in my apartment, I ditched the box, kicked off my heels, and dug into my General Tso's while I checked my mail. The usual new-apartment junk: offers to switch my Internet service provider, cleaning services, credit cards. Not even a catalog to distract me from the task at hand.

I could, perhaps, devote a little time to setting up the rest of my apartment, but I'd already decorated most of the available wall space. One of the downsides of leaving New Jersey for New York was getting used to Manhattan square footage. Not that my lack of real estate mattered much. I might be paying a huge chunk of my pathetic salary on a closet, but it could be a storage unit for all I utilized it. I wasn't exactly throwing dinner parties here. I wasn't even throwing weekend stay-cations with a dedicated lover.

And with that thought, I finished up the rest of my supper and ditched the carton it came in. Okay, that was a nice break. Now back to work.

But two days and eighty-six audition tapes later, I was beginning to wonder exactly how many photographs of my feet I'd have to give Paul McVee in order to get him back. How much groveling would I be able to force myself to pull off in order to keep the show from falling apart?

This evening, I was reviewing audition reels with Lenny via phone. Wife and kids or no, sometimes the guy was going to need to work late.

"The sports guy from St. Louis isn't bad," said Lenny, "Let's watch him again—"

"No," I said. "We need some gravitas."

"Colleen doesn't give us that?"

"We need people to trust us," I continued, ignoring the crack. "If something breaks on air, we need to be able to cover it credibly."

Lenny chuckled. "You think we can actually cover breaking news. God, that's cute."

"Get ready," I said. "'Cause it's going to turn a lot more serious. I will make this show a contender, or die trying."

"I'm coming to believe that." He sighed. "Hold on a minute, I gotta say good night to the kids."

"Thank them for lending me their father tonight. I'm sorry to be keeping you busy so late."

"Will do."

While Lenny saw to his familial duties, I went back to the tapes. The goober from Sacramento. The plastic surgery victim from Miami. This guy from Pittsburgh . . . wait. I didn't remember Pittsburgh. I stuck in the tape. A snowy landscape popped up, along with a young reporter wearing a long wool coat and a scarf wrapped almost up to his nose.

"Thousands gathered around to see if the small creature would see his own shadow," mumbled the reporter through his scarf. He peered at the screen, as if struggling to see something written behind the camera. "And, sadly for us," he went on at last, "according to Punxsutawney Phil, this bitter winter is far from over."

But this dude's audition was. I leaned forward to press "Eject."

"Back to you, Mike," the guy said, as the video cut to the head desk at the studio. The anchor was Mike Pomeroy, who, for just a second, flashed a smirk and rolled his eyes.

I laughed.

"I'm back," came Lenny's voice in my ear. "What's funny?"

"Yesterday," said Mike, his demeanor switching right back to somber, "the State Department held a top-level security briefing on the proliferation of nuclear weapons in rogue states."

"Um . . . did I miss anything brilliant?"

I paused the DVD. On the screen, Mike Pomeroy held a news sheet and looked gravely into the camera.

"Becky?"

I studied the image of Mike Pomeroy, a glimpse of a real newscaster tacked on the end of the audition tape of a wannabe. The juxtaposition wasn't doing Punxsutawney Putz any favors.

"Earth to Becky," Lenny said as Mike began interviewing the secretary of state. "You there? What was so funny? Did you put Seabiscuit back on?"

"No," I said, as Mike grilled the official about enriched uranium. "But I think I found a thoroughbred."

And I hurried right out to share the news. Jerry Barnes's secretary said her boss was attending some charity event at the Met, and I found him, tuxedo-clad and impatient, waiting to enter with his impeccably preserved blond wife. He was, it turned out, totally unimpressed by my brain wave.

"You have to be kidding me." He looked at his wife, who started tapping her designer heels against the pavement. "I'm beginning to suspect that Oscar's sending you to me was some sort of practical joke."

"You have Pomeroy under contract already, right?" I argued. "It wouldn't cost anything."

"It wouldn't necessarily solve anything, either," said Jerry. "He's useless."

"He's a world-caliber newsman."

"He was supposed to do stories for our magazine shows," said Jerry. "We couldn't use anything he pitched us."

"Nothing?" I asked. Not utilize the hell out of the likes of Mike Pomeroy?

Jerry's expression turned sour. "An eight-part series about the United Nations, an interview with a Pashtun warlord, a piece on microfinancing in Asia? Come on. Who cares?"

Well, no one . . . *yet.* But they hadn't heard it the way only Mike Pomeroy could tell the story.

Jerry's wife went from heel-tapping to pointed sighs of impatience. "Jerry—"

He held up a finger. "One second."

"Of course it will be," she drawled, unconvinced. She leveled the stink eye in my direction.

"So you're paying him just to sit there?" I asked. "There must be millions left on his contract. A reporter of his talents—"

"Becky," Jerry said. "Is the stress getting to you already?"

"Pomeroy has reported on every major story of the last three decades with integrity and courage. He was your only anchor to go down to Ground Zero that day. I looked at his Q ratings. They're unbelievable. And you're already paying him."

Jerry looked at me for a long moment, as if assessing the degree to which he thought I'd gone nuts. "I have to go," he said at last, turning to walk away. "We can discuss this in the office tomorrow."

"I want to look at his contract," I insisted. "But I need your approval to do that. Just let me see if there's something there. Please."

Jerry paused.

"Come on," I wheedled. "What have you got to lose?"

He faced me again. "No, the correct question is what have *you* got to lose? I'm going to go inside to this charity dinner. My wife bought a table worth a year of tuition at that college you never bothered to graduate from. Maybe if you had taken a few more broadcasting courses, you would have learned that you can't run a show without an anchor. Maybe you'd have figured out how much lower your precious morale gets when you're running one without an anchor."

How much worse *could* it get? And I felt like I should point out to him that we still had Colleen. Though of course, it couldn't stay that way. I didn't need to go to college to know that morning shows needed two hosts—that the banter was a big reason the audience tuned in. But that wasn't Jerry's point, and it didn't solve my problem anyway. Better I just make nice and get what I want.

"*I'm* going to drink rail liquor and act charitable all night. And *you* want to spend the evening looking over a contract that, even if you can find your precious loophole in it, isn't going to do you any good, because there is absolutely no way that Mike Pomeroy is going to help your morning show. And that show needs help. Desperately."

I swallowed. Make nice. Make nice, make nice, make nice.

"So I should say no," Jerry went on. "Because what you really need to be doing right now is either finding someone new from one of the affiliates, or finding some way to woo back Paul McVee. It might involve a push-up bra."

I crossed my arms over my chest. *Make nice.* "You *should* say no?" I repeated.

"Yes."

"But you're going to say yes?" I refrained from clapping my hands.

"I just did, didn't I?" He whipped out his BlackBerry to send in the order for Mike's contracts. "Hail Mary, Becky Fuller. But either way, you get an anchor in there by Monday or you're through."

"Yes!" I cried. "I will! Thank you!"

Mrs. Barnes rolled her eyes at both of us.

7

had it on good authority that ever since Mike Pomeroy had
started getting money for nothing on his IBS contract, he'd
stepped up his hunting schedule. Apparently all the rumors
about his guns were truth. Today, his quarry was the pheasants
on a small farm outside the city. Hardly my old stomping
ground. No, I liked my meat packaged in convenient con-
tainers made of Styrofoam and plastic wrap. Mike obviously
liked his still wrapped in feathers.

Quite an interesting hobby for a guy who'd once gone ten
rounds with the head of the NRA on live TV. Though I supposed that he made allowances for hunting tools that he
didn't for assault rifles. There was also a decided difference between shooting game and shooting people.

Perhaps I should have donned one of those bright orange
vests?

I found Mike Pomeroy down by the river, clad in a muddied

field jacket with worn elbows and clutching a shotgun. His face was upturned as he scanned the mottled gray sky for pheasants.

The field was pockmarked with rocks and divots in the soil, which made it hard to pick my way across the soft, muddy turf. I should have considered sneakers for this little errand. Oh well, too late now. Besides, I doubted Mike Pomeroy cared about appropriate footwear.

Though you never saw him from the waist down on TV. He could be addicted to wearing huaraches, for all I knew.

"Excuse me, Mr. Pomeroy?"

He whirled around, gun in hand, and I jumped back. All of a sudden, he bore a much closer resemblance to the armed soldiers he'd been embedded with in Afghanistan than to the besuited nightly news anchor.

"Who the hell are you?" he growled. "You're going to scare the birds!"

"I'm Becky Fuller," I said quickly, raising my hands in surrender. "We met the other day in the elevator?"

"Nope." He returned his attention to the sky.

Well, maybe it would be a benefit to me that he couldn't recall my humiliation. I took a deep breath and tried not to think of Dick Cheney and the statistics of accidental shootings. "I'm the producer at *Daybreak*, and, um, we're looking for a new anchor at the moment."

"Then what," he asked without looking at me, "are you doing here?"

"It's funny you should ask—"

He spun and marched off. "Go away."

"Just hear me out." I followed him. "The show has a lot of potential."

He snorted.

"We're starting over, basically. With an anchor as esteemed and respected as you—"

"Go away, go away, go away," Mike said, still looking up.

Since I was practically a foot shorter than him, I didn't know what to do to get his attention back. Grow wings, maybe? Perhaps if I'd rented a plane and done a flyover. The sky banner could have read: "Hey, Mike: Ever thought of *Daybreak*? Call Becky!"

Or not.

"And we're putting together a new format, some—"

"Hey, fangirl," Mike whispered, and stopped.

I smiled at him expectantly. So he *did* remember me from the elevator. Maybe he was even flattered?

"I said *go away*." He took aim and fired his gun into the sky. I shrieked.

"You'd better hope I got it." He took off toward a nearby thicket and I trotted to keep up, more than a little worried that the next time Mike's shotgun went off, he'd be pointing it at something without feathers.

"Look," I said as we shuffled through the leaves and Mike checked under branches and bushes to find the bird. "You've been a journalist all your life, since your elementary-school paper. The *Beaverton Bee*."

"What are you?" he said, pausing momentarily to stare at me. "Some kind of stalker?"

No, I was into news. I knew how to research. Well, I knew how to Google, at least. "You've got to miss reporting. News breaks—it must kill you not to be out there."

Mike leaned into the rushes and snatched out a dead pheasant. I averted my eyes.

"It might," he said. "But you're not out there either, since morning shows *don't. Do. News.*" He twisted the neck of the bird. I heard a pop, and grimaced.

I had informed someone I was coming out here, right? Now, there was some serious news. I mean, if someone were to find the mangled body of a morning show producer in the woods after she pissed off a famous former news anchor with a shotgun. The look on Mike's face was dark enough to make me wonder if that was truly outside the realm of possibility.

"*Daybreak*—Jesus." He stuck the dead pheasant inside his jacket and kept walking. "Half the people who watch your show have lost their remote, and the other half are waiting for the nurse to turn them over."

"But all four of those guys are very loyal viewers," I said.

He stopped and gave me an appraising look. I dared to crack a smile, and for a moment, I thought he might listen. Then he shook his head and walked on.

I kept following him as he left the thicket and hiked back to the boardwalk. I wondered if the pheasant in his coat was bleeding all over his shirt. I wondered if it was still warm. "You don't have to tell me that we don't have the numbers. That's why I think we need you. I think you'd be a real draw for the audience that we'd like to see tuning in to *Daybreak*. And face it, when done right, morning shows can draw huge audiences—"

"If I wanted to come back," said Mike, "I could get any job I wanted."

"But you can't work for another network for two more years," I reminded him.

"And so in the meantime, I'll enjoy my life on IBS's dime." He hefted his gun and gestured to the overcast view of field and stream. There was also a little bit of remarkably smelly swamp.

Wouldn't most people have been enjoying that life on some sandy-white Caribbean beach? No, I had Pomeroy's number. If he wasn't interested in doing some news, he wouldn't have been hanging out at the IBS office that day. He was sniffing around for work—news work.

I knew exactly what that felt like.

Mike's scowl, however, showed he didn't find in me a kindred spirit. "Least those jackasses could do after disbanding the best news department in history and shit-canning me for no reason."

My brow furrowed. "No reason? What about calling the secretary of defense a douche?"

Mike raised a hand in protest. "He lied to an entire nation—"

"He's a politician," I argued. "You've met those before, right?"

"—And, more important," said Mike, "he lied to my face."

I conceded the point, but just as Mike was about to move on, I took a deep breath and stepped in front of him. "Okay. I didn't want to have to do this. I really didn't."

"So don't."

"I went through your contract with the lawyers. And you're right. They have to pay you for the last two years. Unless—"

He gave me a look that made me start envisioning those CSI scenes again. But I braved my way through the terror.

"—Unless six months have elapsed without you appearing on the air in any capacity. And then if the network comes to you with an official offer and you don't take it, they can terminate your contract."

Was that click I heard Mike taking the safety off his shotgun? Do shotguns have safeties?

"And the six million dollars you have left on it," I finished.

The expression on Mike Pomeroy's face was truly terrifying. I'd seen it before. It was the one he'd worn when he interviewed the priest who'd stolen the parishioners' retirement funds. The one he'd leveled at the manufacturer putting lead in baby toys. The one he'd used to bring the isolationist cult leader to tears on live TV.

I straightened and tugged at the hem of my jacket. "So here's me with an official offer: Mike Pomeroy, the IBS network is offering you the position of cohost of *Daybreak*."

Yeah, he was going to kill me. At least it would make a good story for the team at *Good Morning, New Jersey*. Chip would probably win a Pulitzer.

"You can't do this to me."

I lifted my chin, though I was pretty sure those hazel eyes of his were burning right through the back of my skull. "Yes I can."

"Do you have any idea what's going on in the world right now? Do you know what kind of career I've had? And you want me to do stories on Baked Alaska?"

"I—"

"I don't ever want to say the word 'Alaska' on television unless it's followed by one of three things." He held up his fingers to count them off. "Pipeline, earthquake, or governor." He looked at his third finger. "Actually, not even that last one. I'm tired of it."

"You just have to be a little bit open-minded," I said. "Sure, the morning news has a wider range of stories than—"

"'Wider range,'" Mike interrupted. "Nice euphemism." He leaned in. "Your show is in the *news* department—don't you get that? News is a sacred temple, and you, Becky Fuller, are part of the cabal that's ruining it with *horseshit*."

I faltered. Mike Pomeroy had just called my entire career horseshit. I caught my breath, feeling like I'd been punched. This wasn't supposed to be how it happened. The Mike Pomeroy I knew would never use a word like "horseshit."

Of course, the Mike Pomeroy I knew was broadcasting through the little box in my living room, not standing in front of me in the flesh. If he used a word like that on air, the FCC would slap him down with a huge fine. I was very quickly learning that the face Mike Pomeroy showed to the world had about as much to do with the real man as the Barbie doll Colleen Peck liked to portray.

"That's not fair," I said to him, almost before I realized it. "The first half hour of a morning show is a damned good news broadcast."

"Half an hour," said Mike. "Be still my heart."

"And we also do entertainment, weather—everything a newspaper has always done. What's wrong with that?"

Mike shook his head in disgust, shouldered his rifle, and sidestepped me.

I kept up. "We're like a well-informed neighbor, coming over to chat with people in the morning—"

He walked faster. I matched his pace.

"Brokaw did the morning news," I pointed out. "And Charlie Gibson."

"Hmph."

"Walter Cronkite did it at the beginning of his career. He cohosted a morning program with a puppet named Charlemagne—"

Mike stopped dead. Awesome: I'd finally gotten to him. I knew that dropping Cronkite into the discussion would do the trick.

He glared at me. "Then," he said, his voice very low, "*get a puppet.*"

Hmm. Maybe not.

The next morning, I reflected on how it might be a good thing that Mike hadn't taken me up on my offer. After all, I'd tried to sell him a bill of goods about *Daybreak*'s being a great place for the occasional hard-hitting news story. But what were we covering today?

Papier-mâché.

Papier-freaking-mâché, and if the look on Colleen's face every time the camera cut away was anything to go by, even she was unimpressed with the topic. I doubted she wanted her manicure ruined with little pieces of soggy newsprint. And honestly, I couldn't blame her.

But as always, she had her game face on. She beamed with fabricated fascination at our crafts expert as the woman explained why the *Daybreak* set was littered with strips of paper, bowls of glue and water, and entirely too many lumpy, garishly painted objets d'art.

"What's great about papier-mâché," chirped the crafts expert, whom I was beginning to suspect must be on some kind of heavy-dosage mood elevators, "is that it's inexpensive and it uses things you already have around the house. You can make globes, hats"—Colleen's expression flashed a microsecond of horror at the thought of having papier-mâché touch her blond coif—"even piñatas!"

"Wow, piñatas!" Colleen smiled broadly for the camera. "Now, '*macher*' means 'to chew' in French, but we're not going to eat any of this, right?"

"Of course not," said the crafts expert. They both started laughing inanely. I made a note to kill jokes even half as stupid as that one.

"Coming up next," Colleen said. "You've heard her sing. Well, today we're going to hear about her sweet tooth. Join us as we bake brownies with Celine Dion's personal chef."

I wondered if anyone out there was buying the idea that Celine Dion would willingly ingest a brownie.

"All that and more, coming up on *Daybreak*." As the camera light switched off, Colleen's smile was replaced with a look of pure disgust. "Someone get this off me!" she said, flinging out her goop-covered hands. A prop manager rushed forward with a packet of wipes.

"Okay," I said, joining her on the set. "We don't have time for a sit-down on the last piece, so we'll just run the package—"

"You okay?" Colleen stretched out her freshly cleaned hand as if in comfort.

"Excuse me?"

"Don't beat yourself up." Colleen's tone was dismissive. "You were never going to get him. We all know that."

Huh?

She caught my expression. "Pomeroy," she clarified.

"How did you know about that?"

"Everyone knows," she said. "You fired my coanchor. You don't think I've been keeping tabs on what other trained monkey you plan to bring in here?"

"Mike Pomeroy's not a—"

"True, but he wasn't going to come and work at this little dog and pony show, either. Especially not when he'd have to work for someone like . . . well, you."

"Gee, thanks."

"Don't get me wrong," Colleen said, checking out her nails to see how much damage her arts and crafts had wrought. "He was a bold choice on your part. I, for one, would have welcomed him with open arms, but—"

She stopped dead and stared over my shoulder. I suddenly noticed that the entire studio had gone still. Had the camera gone live? Were we sharing this little conversation with the population of the world—or at least, with the few who tuned in to the show?

But no. I turned, and there stood Mike Pomeroy, as out of place on the *Daybreak* set as a wild animal in the middle of Park Avenue.

He was making my staff every bit as skittish, too. I slowly walked over to him.

He spoke without preamble. "I've won eight Peabodies, a Pulitzer, sixteen Emmys, I was shot through the forearm in Bosnia, pulled Colin Powell from a burning jeep, put a washcloth on Mother Teresa's forehead during a cholera epidemic, had *lunch* with Dick Cheney."

"You're here for the money," I said.

"That is correct."

I extended my hand, and Mike grudgingly shook it. "So," I asked, as the stage manager started counting back down to on air, "do you happen to have footage of that thing with Mother Teresa? It would make great promo."

Colleen gaped at us. "Oh, *fuck*."

The camera's on-air light went hot. She snapped into her stage persona, smiling like butter wouldn't melt in her mouth and addressing our four viewers. "Welcome back to *Daybreak*, folks."

Welcome back, I thought, *and don't touch that remote. Things are about to get interesting.*

. . .

"I've taken the liberty of bringing along this rider to my contract," Mike said, handing me a not-insignificant stack of papers.

"A . . . rider?" I stuttered.

Still on air, Colleen did her best to read from the teleprompter while eavesdropping on our conversation.

"Of course," said Mike. "After all, you're forcing me into this through the terms of my contract. I thought I'd return the favor."

"I see." I flipped through. Ten pages. *Ten.* Lenny was going to kill me.

"Please note those are champagne mangoes there on page six," Mike said, practically cheerful. "Not Haden. Way too stringy for my tastes."

"Mangoes," I repeated blankly. And leather furniture on page three. And was this . . . a budget for neckties?

"Which way to my dressing room?" Mike Pomeroy asked. *This had better be worth it,* I warned myself.

"Stay tuned," said Colleen, a little too quickly, "for tips on how you, too, can fight the battle of the bulge."

I wondered if those tips included tropical fruit?

The next few hours were eaten up in a whirlwind of activity as Lenny, the *Daybreak* assistants, and all the interns we could round up scuttled around trying to redo Paul's dressing room—step one: jettison the cot—and fulfill the terms of Mike's ridiculous rider. I knew that every last one of them would spend the evening complaining to their significant other over a glass of beer.

I didn't care. Even if I had a significant other, this would be the first time since I took the *Daybreak* gig that he wouldn't hear me whining. I'd bagged *Mike Pomeroy*. He was going to anchor my show.

My. Show.

"My show," Colleen said to me as soon as she was off the air. "What are his demands, exactly? My past anchors and I have always had a pretty equitable split when it came to what topics we cover. Is he going to cook? Do fashion segments? Gossip?" She flung out her hands. "Papier-mâché?"

"Well . . . ," I said. We were walking down the hall toward her dressing room, and I was trying to keep her rant to a low roar, at least until we were safely behind closed doors.

"Is he going to have three-year-old octuplets barf on him like I did last year?" she wailed.

I ushered her into her dressing room. "Colleen," I said. "The thing I respect most about you is what a team player you are."

"Oh God." She plopped down on the chair in front of her vanity. "I don't like where this is going."

"And you know as well as I do that Mike Pomeroy is going to raise the profile of this show a great deal."

"So I'm chopped liver, that's what you're saying." Colleen spun in her chair and looked in the mirror. "Maybe if I had crow's-feet and a penis and had pulled Mother Teresa out of a burning jeep or whatever . . ."

"Colin Powell in the jeep. Mother Teresa in the cholera epidemic."

"Colonel Mustard in the library with a revolver!" said Colleen with a wave of her hand. "Who gives a shit! Don't tell me—millions of viewers, right?"

"One can only hope," I said.

"You know what I hate?" she said. "That male anchors can keep getting old and what they gain is 'gravitas.'" She made air quotes. "What I gain is falling Q ratings."

I gave a sympathetic head nod.

"I'm a journalist too, you know," she said.

Of sorts. But now was the time for mollification, not explaining to Colleen the difference between a Pulitzer winner and a pageant queen. "Here's the thing. Back in the eighties, someone gave him story refusal rights, so—"

Colleen paused in the midst of checking her eyelids for forbidden creases. "You're kidding me. He does know this is *morning* television, right?"

"I'm sure," I said, hoping I sounded far more convinced than I felt, "that over time, he'll want to do a broad range of stories."

Colleen laughed mirthlessly. "Face it, I'm going to be making turkey meatballs with Mario Batali for the rest of my natural life. Fantabulous."

Ooh, could we get Mario? That would be a huge step up from Celine Dion's dude.

8

ogically, I should have been flying high. After all, I'd gotten exactly what I wanted. My own show. On a network. Hosted by my favorite television reporter of all time. It was Becky Fuller's Christmas wish, all wrapped up with a big red bow.

But Mike Pomeroy seemed determined to make me pay through the nose for it.

The rider? Ridiculous. Story approval, promo approval, champagne-freaking-mangoes! His dressing room demands alone were going to eat into the budget surplus I'd allocated for the new sound mixer. I guess I was going to have to give up one of my three pennies in order to get the show I wanted. But if it worked . . . oh, if it worked, it would all be worth it.

I hoped.

Mike was as disgusted with the state of the studio as I'd been baffled by it on my first day.

"How do you guys manage not to get lost down here?" he asked, as I gave him the not-so-grand tour.

I sidestepped a cable. "You'll be surprised how quickly it becomes second nature."

He looked unconvinced.

"Your digs in Bosnia were nicer, I take it?" I asked.

"Oh, I see," he said. "You're comparing your mid-Manhattan television studio with a war-torn, bombed-out nation that suffered a mass genocide. Not only apt, but incredibly sensitive as well."

Point taken. "You're here to make news, Mike, not for a spa vacation."

"I'm here to make an ass of myself on national television," he corrected.

"Six million dollars," I singsonged.

He sighed. "Did you at least install the wet bar?"

I ignored that and kept going. "Colleen's dressing room is at the end of the hall. She's really been looking forward to seeing you."

This was not precisely the case, but neither was it an out-and-out lie. Like all employees of *Daybreak*, Colleen was relieved to see that we'd filled the cohost position. She just wasn't thrilled about the package it came in. I wanted to shut them both in a room until they hashed it out, but I feared that the bloodbath would necessitate my finding *two* new hosts.

"Great," Mike said. "Happy to hear it."

Really? I smiled in surprise. Oh, good, maybe this would work out after all. I paused in front of Colleen's dressing room. Mike kept going.

"Um . . ." I pointed at Colleen's door. Mike stopped in front of his.

"This one mine?"

"Yes," I said. "But Colleen is waiting—"

Mike opened the door and surveyed his new domain. I trailed after him.

"You got me all the newspapers," he said approvingly. "And the mixers. And the tropical fruit plate. I hope you remembered the mango situation."

"Well," I said, my tone dry, "you were pretty clear in your rider."

He sat down on the nearest chair, rested his feet on the vanity, and picked up a bunch of lychees. "If Colleen wants me, I'll be right here. Pass the *Washington Post*, would you? I've already seen the *Times*."

"But—"

"Right. Here." He raised his eyebrows, then turned his attention to the newspaper.

I hurried back to Colleen.

"Where's Mike?" she asked.

"Oh," I said lightly. "In his dressing room. Let's go over and say hi."

No go. Colleen looked at me like I was crazy. "I thought he was coming in here to meet me."

"Oh, well . . ." I searched around for an excuse. "He's just getting settled in, you know? Wouldn't it be nice if you just dropped by to welcome him to the —"

"No," she stated. "He should come in here."

Right. I nodded and turned on my heel.

Back at Mike's, I found him exploring the papaya and an article on Yemen.

"Hey, Mike," I said, imbuing my words with a casual bonhomie I did not feel, "what's up?"

"I was thinking," he said, "about the paint color in here. Not very relaxing, is it?"

"It's beige," I said flatly.

"Mmmmm." He held up the skin of the mango. "What about something more like this?"

I glared at him. "You want a reputation as a diva around this network, Mike? I can make that happen."

"No you can't," he replied. "And you wouldn't, even if you could."

He had me there. "Okay," I said. "We can discuss paint colors after you see Colleen. I think you'll love what she's done to *her* dressing room."

"Nah," he said. "I think I'll stay right here. She can come in and tell me about her room if she wants."

I resisted the urge to stamp my foot like a toddler.

"No hurry," he added, and returned to his paper.

I headed back to Colleen's.

She met me at the door. "*No.*"

And, back to Mike's. He took one look at my frustrated face and almost burst out laughing. "Did you tell her I had *papaya* in here?"

I reminded myself that Mike Pomeroy was one of the best newscasters in history as I clomped my way back to Colleen's dressing room to relay the papaya message. As if it would do any good.

"He has a *tropical fruit plate?*" Colleen shrieked. "That is so typical! I'm the one doing all the work around here, and I'm the one with the smaller room, the smaller salary, the smaller—"

"Ego?" I suggested mildly. "You're right. You work hard. And right now, I'm just asking you to—"

"I can't believe he's pulling rank like this." She tossed her head and then checked her reflection in the mirror. "And it's a little odd that he won't deign to meet me now. He was plenty keen on the idea at the last Correspondents' Dinner."

"Excuse me?"

"Yeah!" cried Colleen. "When he grabbed my ass and asked me if I wanted to go back to his hotel room for a little—"

I threw my hands in the air. "Enough! I don't need to hear any more."

"Because he's your *hero?*" Colleen said with a sneer.

"Because he's being a big baby, and so are you." I sighed. "Look, he's an asshole. I'm with you there. But you, my dear, are the host of a morning show that last week got beaten by a rerun of *Sanford and Son* on TV Land."

"You're kidding." But she sounded defeated.

"Unfortunately for you, and even more unfortunately for me, we're going to have to put up with him, because asshole or not, he's *our only hope.* So I suggest you man up and get in there."

The look she gave me at the words "man up" reminded me that not only had she already survived half a dozen male anchors, but that we were currently kowtowing to the childish behavior of yet another.

"Nice speech," said Colleen. "But I'm not going in there. Figure something else out."

Easier demanded than done. I stood in the hall between the dressing rooms of my feuding cohosts, and tried to come up with options. A prop guy walked by. "Hey," I called to him. "You have any marking tape?"

Five minutes later, ten steps from Mike's room and ten steps from Colleen's, standing on a pair of twin phosphorescent Xs, the cohosts of *Daybreak* stood like the petulant children they were and stared at me while I did a rundown of the week's schedule.

"We'll be shooting Mike's promos all this week, and on Friday, we'll finalize the new format. We'll need to rehearse the opening, of course, and some segues."

"Who's going to say goodbye?" asked Colleen.

"I beg your pardon?" I blinked at her.

"At the end of the show," she clarified.

I shrugged. "Doesn't matter. I don't care." I looked at Mike, who'd avoided even glancing at Colleen throughout the entire conversation. Surely, a newsman of his stature wouldn't quibble over such a little thing either. "Mike, you don't—"

"I've always said it." Mike studied his nails.

"Oh no," said Colleen. "I've been saying it for the last eleven years. My audience expects certain things from me and—"

"Who do you think the public would rather hear from last?" asked Mike. "Someone who's won every broadcasting honor on the face of the planet . . . or the former Miss Pacoima?" And then he marched right back into his dressing room and slammed the door.

"Arizona!" Colleen shouted after him. "I was Miss *Arizona!*"

And I was getting a headache.

When the staff convened for Mike's introductory meeting, I noticed a few of the younger producers getting that same starry-eyed look I'd had the first time I met Pomeroy in the flesh.

I wondered how long the illusion would last for *them.*

I stood at the end of the conference table, in front of a huge dry erase board covered with the schedule of stories for the week. Here at least, I was back in my element. Wrangling divas wasn't my thing. Making a news show happen? That I adored.

"Okay," I said, pointing at the board. "So we've got the Bird Whisperer confirmed for Tuesday—thanks, Sasha."

The producer nodded. I'd already learned she was the animal lover on staff. If I ever needed a stupid pet trick to round out the show, Sasha was my go-to gal.

"Wednesday we've got Al Green outside on the plaza. . . . Colleen, you want to do the interview with him between songs?"

"Oh no, let me," Mike deadpanned.

Colleen scowled, saving me the trouble. "Fine," she said. "Whatever."

I put a red C next to the Al Green slot. "And then, we're doing that piece on water safety for children. . . ."

"Not my thing," said Mike.

Another red C. "There's the rundown of the new shows on the fall television season. . . ."

"Oh, yeah," said Mike. I brightened. "That's a no."

I slumped. "Special Olympics?"

His eyebrow crooked. "What do you think?"

Everyone in the room looked from him to me, but if they were expecting a repeat of my behavior toward Paul McVee, they could keep on living in fantasyland. I needed a host, even if he was being a bitch about it.

"Well," I said halfheartedly, "Newt Gingrich just wrote a book. We weren't going to do an interview, but—"

"Oh, I'll do that," said Mike, sitting up in his chair. "I'd love to fry that jackass."

"Um . . . ," I said, taken aback. "I guess that's . . . okay. . . ."
I put a blue M next to Gingrich.

Out of the corner of my eye, I caught Colleen's expression.
Pissed. Then Lenny's. A mix of surprise and disappointment.
Then Mike's.

Smug bastard.

After the meeting, Lenny met me out by the Craft Services table. The donuts, I noticed, were the same ones as ever.

"What's up, boss?" Lenny asked me. "You hired this guy to do what? One story a week?"

"What do you want me to do?" I asked, exasperated. I began piling pastries on a plate. Problems like this called for plenty of butter and sugar. "I can't fire another anchor, unless we want to get stuck with the guy who counts on his hooves."

"And you can't make Colleen do every story on the docket, either."

"He's Mike Pomeroy," I said. "A legend. Who am I to tell him what to do?"

Lenny didn't say anything. He didn't have to. Right: I was the executive producer. And if the dude who ululated his way through this job thought something was off in my performance, I needed some serious help.

Just then, the legend himself came sauntering up, smacking loudly on an apple. I doubted horse face could have outperformed him. He gave me a long, appraising look.

I stood even straighter. Maybe he'd been impressed by my leadership skills at the meeting. Maybe he was rethinking his campaign of punishment for forcing him onto the show. Maybe we could finally get a real working relationship started.

"It's interesting Jerry hired you," he said.

Maybe not. "Oh yeah?"

"Yeah." He took another bite. "No polish, no pedigree, that haircut. What was he thinking?"

I narrowed my eyes and put another Danish on my towering plate. Fine, Mike, play it that way if you want. Be as rude as you want, as difficult as you want, as ornery as you want. You're still going to sit on *my* set and read *my* news on *my* show.

"Just wondering," he finished, and then, without looking, he tossed the apple core into the trash behind me. "Score," he said, pumping his fists in the air. He grinned and walked off.

Score indeed. I watched him go. *Okay, alpha dog. You've made your point.* But I would not let him walk all over me. If he thought he could piss me off enough to fire him, he was wrong.

Mike Pomeroy's criticisms might be bad for my morale, but he was still good for *Daybreak*.

"Sweet guy," said Lenny. "One wonders how he ever got such a bad reputation."

"You mean that he's tough to deal with when it comes to stories?" I asked. "He just has high standards."

Lenny shook his head. "No way. There's this guy he used to work with up at *Nightly News*? Says he made his life hell."

"Adam Bennett?" I asked, remembering what the cute producer had told me the day I met him in the elevator.

"Oh, him too?" Lenny said.

Too? Shit.

Mike and I next clashed swords after filming his promos. We sat in the editing room, going over all the clips we had prepared. I wanted to advertise the hell out of his new position.

People missed Mike Pomeroy on *Nightly News*. If they found out they could see him in the morning, even on *Daybreak*, it might bring in his old fans.

Especially if he was spending most of his mornings frying Newt Gingrich.

Except right now, Mike Pomeroy seemed satisfied to sit in a dark room watching promo clips and frying me.

"Okay," I said wearily. "What about this one?"

A shot of the courthouse came up, then a close-up on Mike's ruggedly handsome face. "Coming soon to *Daybreak*," boomed the voice-over, "one of the most legendary newsmen of all time."

On the screen, Mike trotted up the courthouse steps carrying a briefcase and looking like a refugee from a John Grisham film.

"Oh for Christ's sake," said one of the most legendary newsmen of all time. He leaned back in his chair. The film editor, who looked like he might burst into flames if his skin was ever exposed to natural light, paused the recording as the *Daybreak* logo sparkled its way across the scene.

"What now?" I asked.

"It's embarrassing," said Mike, gesturing at the screen. "Like that briefcase. What the hell do I have in there? Special anchorman papers?"

"We've been over this *eight* times," I said, as the editor yawned and pressed "ESC."

"Plus, I'm on my way to nowhere," Mike said. "There's not even a door on that side. I look like a jackass."

"No one is going to look that hard," said the editor, but Mike shut him up with a single stone-cold glance. "Sorry, sir."

"You know," I said, "whoever gave you promo approval was smoking crack."

Mike shrugged. "I was mopping the floor with Peter Jennings at the time. I could have gotten hookers and eight-balls written into my contract if I wanted."

"And you settled for champagne mangoes?" I replied. "Sucker."

The editor started again.

"Okay, this one you'll like," I said. A shot popped up of Mike sitting at the anchor desk as the voice-over extolled his legendary status.

"You wrote this copy, right, fangirl?" said Mike.

I ignored him.

"Soon," said the voice-over, "he'll be bringing his experience to morning television." The shot switched to one of Mike walking purposefully *into* the IBS building.

I gave him a triumphant look. "See? This time there's a door."

The voice-over went on. "Let Mike Pomeroy show you the world over your first cup of coffee."

And . . . *Daybreak*. Sparkle, sparkle.

I turned to him, smiling expectantly.

Mike groaned. "'Your first cup of coffee'? Do we really have to mention that? Why don't we just say, 'Watch Mike Pomeroy before you take your morning dump'?"

The editor snickered. I nearly growled.

9

After finally hammering out a promo the great Mike Pomeroy could live with, I trudged back to my office. What had I gotten myself into? Maybe after he figured I was sufficiently punished for forcing him into the job, he'd settle down. I hoped I hadn't made a huge mistake with this guy.

I was so lost in my own thoughts, I almost ran into Adam Bennett, who was waiting for me outside my office. Today, he looked a little spruced up. At least, his shirt was tucked in.

"Hey there," he said, grinning. "Just came to offer my condolences on hiring the third-worst person in the world."

I mustered a smile and hoped I wasn't blushing. "Yeah, well, you may have had a point there."

"Everyone upstairs is wondering what you're thinking."

I opened the door to my office and he followed me inside.

"Everyone upstairs is still talking about this show? Good, my evil plan is working."

He chuckled.

"Meant to ask you," I said, dropping my files onto my desk, "who are the first two worst people in the world?"

"Kim Jong II and Angela Lansbury," said Adam, in all seriousness. "She knows what she did."

"So," I said. "You worked with Mike at *Nightly News?*"

He nodded. "Worst year of my life. I lost twelve pounds."

Yikes. The guy did not need to lose any pounds: He was pretty much perfect as he was. I watched him check out my office, taking in the bare walls and the piles of paper. I wondered what he had in his office. Golfing trophies, perhaps? Or was he more of a basketball type?

"The entire time we worked together," he said, "the only thing Mike ever called me was Señor Dipshit."

"Harsh." I laughed. "Sorry, that's not funny. It's terrible." And hilarious.

"So now," said Adam, "is an excellent time for you to take up drinking. I came by to tell you that sometimes, after work, a few of us go to Schiller's. You know . . . downtown?"

I didn't, but then, I was a newbie to the island.

"So if you're ever around . . ." He let it hang in the air.

"Oh, great," I said. "I don't go out all that much but—"

I saw Lenny lurking outside my office door.

"Uh . . ." I amended my speech in response to the encouraging look on Adam's face. "But if I'm walking by, I'll stop in and say hi."

"Great!" Adam beamed. "Tomorrow night? Around eight?"

"Oh. Great. Sounds good."

Adam left, leaving me to contemplate my lack of interior

design. Maybe I should get a few photos or something in here. A plant, perhaps? A plastic one, given the lack of sunlight?

Lenny passed by again, this time carrying a copy of our most recent schedule. "Not too bad. You finally nailed down Mike's promo, and you got asked out on a date. Things are looking up."

"What?" I said. "He didn't ask me on a date."

"He did," said Lenny. "I heard him on my way in."

"What? No. He just mentioned he might be somewhere and . . . believe me, I know when I'm being asked on a date, and that was not it."

"Believe me," said Lenny, "I'm a guy. I know the strategy. It was soft serve, yeah, but it was still there."

"Oh, please," I scoffed.

"Okay, we'll see what happens after you go there tomorrow."

I looked at Lenny. He looked at me.

"Because you *are* going there tomorrow."

I narrowed my eyes at Lenny. He narrowed his eyes at me.

Then I shook my head. It was silly. And impossible. I grabbed a notebook off the desk and flipped through it, searching for a subject to switch to. Except that my mind was racing. After all, he didn't need to come all the way down here to tell me Mike Pomeroy was a jerk. I'd figured that out all on my own.

At lunchtime, I met two of my producers at a streetside café down the block from IBS to go over some stories. Sasha, the animal lover, was pitching something on palm oil and how its production was endangering orangutans. A promising story, to be sure, but we needed a hook to make it work for the morning show audience.

"See if you can find a nearby zoo with an orangutan breeding program," I said. "People like baby monkeys. We'll get one on set."

"Orangutans are apes, not monkeys," snipped Sasha.

"Maybe we can get one to poop on Mike Pomeroy," said Tracy, the other producer. She was still bruised by his disparaging comments at our last morning meeting over her fashion week coverage. Though I have to admit, I'd had to hide my snicker when he'd said the last time he cared about the design of a vest was when he was wearing it as body armor in Iraq.

"Work with that," I said to Sasha, then took a bite of my salad. It was a beautiful, sunny day on the streets of New York City, and I was planning a news show with my staff. Issues with Mike and the budget aside, this was still a dream job. As long as I could drum up some more interest in the show, I'd be golden. I turned a page in my notebook and anchored it down with the corner of my plate. Eating outside had its perks, but the last thing I needed was for our news stories to be blown across Madison Avenue.

"Okay, Tracy," I said. "In the fashion segments, I think it's important to interpret runway trends for our viewers."

"We already adjust to their budgets," she said.

"Yeah, but we need to think about more than that. We need to focus our stories on things they'd actually wear. The average woman is not six feet tall and a size zero."

But Tracy had stopped listening. Sasha, also, seemed otherwise occupied. I followed their gazes and saw Adam Bennett crossing the street toward the IBS building.

"Man, he's cute," said Tracy.

"I went to Yale with him," said Sasha.

"You did not!" Tracy practically squealed.

Sasha raised her eyebrows. "Everyone there was madly in love with him, too. Including me."

"Okay, guys," I said, waving my hands in front of their faces. "Can we—"

"Tell me more," Tracy begged Sasha.

"I want to talk about this leggings piece," I tried. "Colleen said that under no circumstances would she put them on her body—"

"His dad was the editor of *Newsweek*," said Sasha, "so naturally all the journos sucked up to him. And his mom's family is rich as hell. They own Tupperware or something."

I sat back, surprised. I barely owned a *piece* of Tupperware.

"He rowed crew when Yale won the national championship—," Sasha was saying.

Just then, Adam spotted me at the café and waved. I waved back, hoping he couldn't see my blush from across the street. *Are your ears burning, Adam?*

Sasha and Tracy slowly looked from him to me. "You . . . know him?" said Tracy.

"Yes," I said. Well, apparently not as well as Sasha did, but yes. So the whole untucked shirt thing was in fact a prep school slacker affectation. Should have known.

"Don't you think he's smokin'?" she asked.

"Smokin'," I repeated. "Lemme see. Sure? I don't know."

They both seemed skeptical. And possibly jealous.

"So," I said. "Back to the top of the show?"

I was more convinced than ever that drinks with Adam and a few of his colleagues was nothing remotely resembling a date, despite Lenny's insistence to the contrary. I wondered what my associate producer's deal was anyway. Was he just one of those happily married guys to whom the thought of a single life was anathema? Or did I come across as pathetic and lonely as I often felt?

Either way, Mr. Yale Crew Tupperware did not have a lot in common with me. He was just being friendly with the new girl. I tried to keep my conversation focused on the show, but I couldn't help sneaking one last peek at Adam as he disappeared inside IBS without a backward glance.

Yep, just being friendly.

My certainty on the subject, however, did not prevent me from dressing with extra care the following day, nor from using the straightening iron, nor from putting on an extra coat of both mascara and lipstick.

But when I looked at myself in the bathroom mirror before heading off to work, I groaned and scrubbed it all off. Might as well scream "Jersey girl," right?

"You look nice," said Sasha at the morning meeting. "Hot date?"

"Cute suit," said Colleen as we prepped for her food segment. "Got a new job interview already?"

"Hey, fangirl," said Mike, "your hair's looking awful big today."

I flattened my bangs and glared at him.

Around seven, Lenny knocked on my office door. "I'm out of here," he said. "Don't forget you've got that 'appointment' at the bar tonight."

"I'm getting scared of you and your odd obsession with my personal life."

He shrugged. "You forget. I had your job, and I know better than anyone else how much someone in that position needs to have an outlet. It's self-preservation, really. I don't want you marching in here one day with a shotgun."

I smirked. No, I'd leave that behavior to Mike Pomeroy.

"So get a boyfriend or a Boston terrier, I don't care, but get out of here."

I waved him off, but as soon as he was gone, I took one last crack at my hair, then grabbed my briefcase and headed out.

Schiller's looked like the illegitimate love child of a French bistro and a subway station. There were a group of people with IBS ID tags clustered near the bar. Adam was among their number, and he spotted me right away.

I put up my hand to wave, and accidentally tossed my BlackBerry across the room. A few of the producers laughed.

Smooth one, Becky.

I was down on my knees looking for it when I spotted Adam's loafer-clad toes. I rose, taking in nicely tailored pants, the ubiquitous untucked dress shirt, and a hint of five o'clock shadow beneath his smiling jaw. He handed me my phone. "Slippery little bugger, huh?" he said. "You look like a woman who needs a drink."

"Yes, please."

Adam waved to the bartender. "Beer?" he asked. "Or are you a hard liquor girl? Please tell me you don't do cosmos."

"Beer is fine," I said.

"For now." Adam waited as I put in my order. "You'll need something stiffer after Mike really starts getting to you."

"Oh, he's getting to me," I said, as the bartender brought my beer. "Usually, I drink Sprite."

Adam laughed. "I almost needed an intervention before I left *Nightly News*."

"So it's better now?"

"Absolutely. Plus, the hours are better at *7 Days*." He grinned at me. "I get to go out now."

Go out. *Go out* go out? Man, he was vague!

"Hey, let's grab a table before this place fills up. Look, there's one."

I glanced at his group of friends. "Oh, don't you want to—"

And then he put his hand on the small of my back, and I completely forgot what I was about to say. He guided me toward the empty booth while my mind raced. So this *was* a date? I mean, I didn't even get a chance to meet those friends of his. Maybe Lenny was right, and he'd . . . lured me here under false pretenses. Got me to come on a date without asking me on a date. Maybe this was how things worked in the Ivy League.

But why would a guy like Adam Bennett need to do that? Wasn't he the sort of person who could just saunter up to a woman and go "Pick you up at eight, baby," and they'd fall all over him? I knew Tracy would. Sasha too, come to think of it.

And . . . me. If he'd actually asked me out, I'd have gone.

So now here he was, seated across from me in a booth, and checking out the description of the nacho platter on the dinner menu.

"Are you hungry?"

I started gulping my beer. Okay, so . . . date.

We ordered some nachos, and chatted about our early jobs in television news. Seemed Adam had come straight to network out of college; I guessed those were the perks that came with the *Newsweek* legacy.

"And you were at some show in Jersey before, right?" he said.

"Yeah." I looked down at my glass. "Then I got ditched for some—" Crap. Some Ivy League rich boy. Hell, Adam and Chip were probably roommates.

"Some . . . ?" Adam prodded.

Blue-blooded, overeducated, nepotistic, old-boys' network-owning, Brooks Brothers–wearing—

"Uh-oh." Adam pulled out his buzzing BlackBerry. "Becky, I'm so sorry, but I have to take this. I've been trying to track down this source all week. It'll just be a second, okay?"

"Okay," I said, relieved on two counts. First, I could come up with a new topic by the time he got back. Second, he was as BlackBerry-mad as me.

As promised, he was back within moments, and, like the seasoned news producer I was, I turned the interview to him. But Adam was apparently every bit as skilled as I was, and repeatedly turned the conversation from anything that had a whiff of "summer house in the Hamptons" to war stories about our days in the newsroom.

"Seriously," he said at last. "How are things going with Mike? All the veterans from *Nightly News* are pulling for you, you know that."

"You mean there's not a pool going on how soon I'll crack?"

"Well, yeah," said Adam, "but those of us with the long odds are hoping you'll last."

I laughed, and we ordered another round as we shared our favorite Mike Pomeroy anecdotes.

"I asked him to do a piece on Trump, and he took my Diet Coke can and hurled it across the room."

"Nice," said Adam, scooping up a bit of guacamole with the last of the nachos. "I asked him to cover a bumper crop of cranberries, he punched me in the face."

"You're kidding," I said.

"To be fair, he was drunk off his ass at the time."

I shook my head. "No excuse. If he tried to punch me in the face, I'd lay him out flat. I'm from New Jersey."

Adam regarded me carefully. "Yeah, I believe it. So, has he given you a nickname yet?"

I paused, a chip halfway to my mouth. "Um . . . sometimes he calls me fangirl."

"Fangirl?" he said.

"Yeah, you know, to underscore the fact that I should be respecting his venerable position and worshipping the ground he walks on."

"Ah, right. Your little performance in the elevator."

I saluted him with my beer.

"Well, it's better than Señor Dipshit." Adam shrugged. "If I didn't know better, I'd say he actually liked you."

"Maybe you don't know better," I said.

"Maybe he likes being worshipped by pretty young things," he replied.

I threw a jalapeño slice at him. Pretty young thing, huh?

We were still laughing when a tall blond girl approached the table. She easily had four inches on me, and that was before you counted her designer heels. Diamond studs the size of blueberries shone from her earlobes, and her outfit was one I remembered being featured on a recent segment about the newest trends from Milan.

"Adam!" she cried, her voice musical.

He looked up. "Oh, hey." He stood and hugged her. They looked like a Ralph Lauren ad. Two perfect specimens of preppy northeastern elite.

"You never called me!" The girl affected a pout.

"Sorry." Adam cast me a sidelong glance. "I've been, um . . . working a lot. . . ."

Working a lot? Oh, I see. This was work. Even Perfect Girl here didn't seem to view the situation as datelike. She made no move to introduce herself to me. Neither did Adam. She started talking about some of the doings in Greenwich. I swirled the dregs of my beer around the bottom of my glass. This was taking considerably longer than Adam's all-important phone call with his source.

Guess Perfect Girl ranked higher on his list of priorities.

"So, I'm in the middle of—"

"Right," said Perfect Girl. "Maybe I'll see you at Barton's regatta party on Saturday?"

Regatta? *Regatta?* Jesus, what was I doing here? The closest I'd ever gotten to a regatta was a story I'd once done at *Good Morning, New Jersey* about a rash of car thefts at the Barnegat Bay Yacht Club.

"Yeah," said Adam. "Great."

"Okay, great," said Perfect Girl. She turned to me. "Nice to meet you."

She hadn't. I almost said this aloud.

"Sorry," she went on, her tone blithe, "I was just so glad to see Adam again—"

"No, it's fine," I said. "Fine, fine, fine." *Oh, God, Becky, shut up. You sound inane.* But my heart was racing, and my palms were damp. What in the world was I doing here next to this Amazonian goddess?

As soon as she was gone, Adam sat down again. "Sorry about that."

"So that's why I came by tonight," I blurted. "Because I don't know that many people who know Mike and I really needed your. . . . professional feedback."

"My . . . feedback?" Adam asked.

"Yeah." I searched around desperately for my scattered

vocabulary. "Well, I'm new in town, and I don't have that many . . . work contacts."

I knew I should also try to find the pieces of my shredded dignity. I needed to get *out* of there. Quickly.

"Great," Adam said slowly. "So we'll be . . . work contacts."

"Exactly."

"Can't have enough of those," he said, his tone flat.

He probably couldn't have enough girlfriends, either. I was at a complete loss as to what to do. This whole evening had just imploded around me. I was going to kill Lenny. I never even would have been thinking in terms of dates if it hadn't been for him and his stupid model wife. He'd made me actually think, for a moment, that it made some kind of strange sense for someone like me to go out with someone like Adam. But of course not. Stupid. Stupid.

The need to bolt became overwhelming.

"Well." I stuck out my hand. "I'll be seeing you around, then. Definitely."

He looked down at my hand, brow furrowed, then shook it. "Okay."

I grabbed my jacket and ran, unable to catch my breath until I hit the street. I stood there for a moment in the fading light, asking myself and God how in the world it was that I could track down gun-toting maniac reporters in the wilds of New Jersey, but couldn't manage to make small talk with a cute guy in a trendy Manhattan bar. Was it some kind of weird brain damage? Had I been dropped on my romance lobe as a child? Did I need behavioral therapy? Most important, could we build a segment around this kind of pathological boy-girl ineptitude? Gah.

I sneaked a peek inside the window of the pub. Adam was

still sitting at our booth, staring down into his beer. He looked as baffled as I felt. And then I saw him reach across the table and pick something up from my side of the table.

My IBS badge. Oh no. Should I go in there and get it? Did I dare show my face in front of him again?

He ran his thumb lightly over my picture on the plastic, and I shivered as if the caress had touched my face. He looked at it one moment more, gave a slight shake of his head, then stuck it in his shirt pocket.

Shit. I'd totally screwed up back there.

10

My IBS badge was waiting for me at the security desk when I arrived the next morning.

"You should really keep more careful track of these," the guard said as I signed the necessary paperwork to retrieve it.

"Yeah," I said, though I wanted to curl up and die. Of course Adam wouldn't have called me to tell me he had it, or even where he was going to put it. I'd just run out the door on him. He probably never wanted to speak to me again. Leaving it here was the low-impact way to return it. It was either that or interoffice mail.

God, how humiliating.

I headed down to the *Daybreak* studios to face the gauntlet of our final rehearsal before Mike's first broadcast. Lenny met me at the office.

"So how was it?" he asked.

"Nuclear disaster," I said, breezing by him to the coffee machine. "I am never listening to you again."

"Really?" Lenny raised his eyebrows. "I'd always heard Adam was a mensch."

"Adam is fine," I said. "I'm Chernobyl."

"I see."

We headed off to rehearsal. I saw the problems coming as soon as I got Mike and Colleen situated behind the anchor desks. Mike started playing with the levers on his chair, adjusting it so he sat a wee bit higher than Colleen.

She glared at him and adjusted her own seat.

I started worrying that the camera was going to show only their feet and told them both to cut it out.

"Okay," I said, bringing their focus back to the actual script. "So the plan is to alternate voice-over intros of the headlines, and then you two ad-lib. So say we have a story about . . . I don't know . . . the midterm elections—"

"We won't, though," Mike pointed out. "Because we don't actually cover the news."

"Pompous," grumbled Colleen. "Gee, that's a different color for you."

I ignored them both. "So you guys should just banter back and forth a little."

" 'Banter'?" Mike said. "From the Latin for 'to gibber like an idiot'?"

I grit my teeth. "Just . . . talk about the headlines. You know what I mean." Come on, Mike, they banter on the nightly news! Was he going to fight me every single step of the way?

"Fine." He stood up and straightened his tie. "I'll do it . . . when we get on the air. I'm not going to sit here and rehearse like I'm in summer stock. I've been on television for forty years—I think I know how to ad-lib."

He hopped down from the set. I turned to Colleen. "Okay," I said. "Then maybe you and I can rehearse."

Colleen rolled her eyes and slipped out of her chair as well.

"Great," I said to no one in particular. "I'm glad we could have this time to . . . I really feel like we're meshing right now. . . ."

I wondered if it was too late to get in on that "When Is Becky Fuller Going to Crack?" pool Adam had mentioned.

When I got back to my office, I heard the special inner-IBS ring tone. My heart leapt. Maybe it was Adam, hoping to give it another try. I checked the readout. Or . . . Jerry.

"Hi, Jerry," I said in my peppiest voice.

"How's it going down there?" he asked.

"Oh, Mike's ready. We've been rehearsing all week." Little white lies.

I carried the phone out to the door of my office. Mike was back at the anchor desk, spinning side to side in the chair and throwing Raisinets at a cameraman who was adjusting the lighting. The cameraman spun around and Mike raised his eyes to the ceiling, whistling innocently.

"He's in . . . great spirits," I finished, miserable.

"That's not what I heard," said Jerry. "I heard you're spending all your time trying to wrangle him. That you barely have time to retool the show."

True and true. And who was Jerry's little spy down here? "Look, all I need to do is get him on the air, okay? The public loves him. Will the show still need fine-tuning? Yes." I took a deep breath, hoping to convince myself as much as my boss:

"But trust me, Jerry—Mike Pomeroy is the key to taking this show where it needs to go."

He'd better be, or I'd break his neck like he was one of those pheasants.

Jerry didn't sound convinced. "Hope you know what you're doing, staking everything on him."

"I'm not worried," I said, braving a smile that I knew he couldn't see. We said our goodbyes, then I walked casually out of my office, down the hall, and into the ladies' room, where I promptly started hyperventilating.

Oh, God, I hoped I knew what I was doing, staking my entire career on him.

By the end of the day, I'd worked myself into a full-fledged panic attack. I vacillated between two trains of thought: My plan was brilliant and I would become a legend in the world of morning news; my plan was poised to become the industry laughingstock. The problem was that there was nothing I could do to influence the outcome at this point. Either Mike would hold it together and be the newscaster I knew he had in him, or he would embarrass us all by treating the show like a cosmic joke.

I had to talk to him. I'd beg if I had to.

I gathered up the material I was taking home to review and marched over to his dressing room.

"Enter!" came floating through the door at my knock.

I opened the door. Mike was in his chair, drinking a scotch and watching the feed monitors.

"Hi," I said, keeping my tone casual. "Just wanted to say good luck tomorrow."

He faced me, then tilted his head to read the label on the DVD in my hand. "Ah, Colleen's pap smear. A classic."

Enough was enough. He wasn't the single arbiter of what belonged on TV. "You know, she may have saved some lives by encouraging women to—"

"My God, this place is absurd." Mike gestured broadly with the hand that held his scotch. "Say what you want about Dan Rather, at least I never had to see his cervix."

I studied him. "Are you drunk?"

"Insufficiently."

He pointed to the feed monitor, which was currently showing the rehearsal for *Nightly News*. The new anchor, Patrick Jameson, was barely forty. He had a St. Barts tan and the smile of a matinee idol. Also, according to rumor, he had the brain of an unusually intelligent shih tzu; but audiences didn't seem to care, since he managed to sound plenty intelligent reading off the prompters.

"The spill began when the tanker was damaged in heavy seas outside of Galveston," Patrick was saying.

Mike sneered.

Patrick was no doubt matching the script point for point. Another reason the network execs loved him—they never had to worry about him going off book and angering the sponsors. "Officials say up to two hundred thousand gallons of crude oil could be deposited in rough seas in the next forty-eight hours. Current weather conditions are complicating efforts to contain the damage amid fears that the oil could be ignited by the ship's engine."

"That's my chair," Mike slurred. "That's where I should be. And they took it away from me, those motherfu—" He slumped.

"Mike, you should go home." I laid a hand on his shoulder. "Get some rest."

He pointed to the bottle of scotch sitting open on his desk. "You see that? Bruichladdich. Forty-year-old Islay single malt. I only drink it when I'm feeling particularly suicidal."

If he committed suicide before the broadcast, I was going to kill him for sure. And that went double if he did it in my studio. "Time to go home," I said firmly. "I'll see you tomorrow. Bright and early!"

"Aye, aye, captain." He gave me a drunken salute.

I shook my head in disgust and departed.

The *Daybreak* offices were empty. Everyone had already gone home for the night, getting as much rest as they could before tomorrow's big premiere. My bags were waiting in my office, but I couldn't seem to bring myself to follow the example set by my staff and head home. I straightened up my already-tidy office and made sure every pen on the desk made a neat parallel line. I looked at my bags. Tapped my foot.

Oh, enough already.

Thirty seconds later, I was in the elevator. Thirty seconds after that, I was deposited on the floor that housed the news division—the "real news" division, as Mike would probably say. Halfway across the floor was a glass door marked "7 Days." I took a deep breath, told myself that I was making up for having acted like an idiot last night, and pushed through.

Adam's office was the third door on the right. I knocked, hoping that he, too, had not gone home for the night. Or back to the bar to meet with Perfect Blond Regatta Girl.

"Come in," he called.

Adam's office was not decorated with golf trophies, or basketball trophies, or even Yale crew team trophies. Instead, his walls were covered with pictures from his latest story—something to do with the Philippines, judging by the thumb-tacked map behind his desk.

"Hi," I said, standing on the threshold and fighting for a lighthearted tone.

Adam's hair was tousled, His face was unreadable. "Hi."

"I just came by to . . . um . . ." I clasped my hands in front of me to keep them still, and my pinkies touched my badge. "Thank you for, uh, returning my ID."

"Figured you couldn't get in without it," he said. He hadn't moved from behind his desk, and his usual easy smile was absent this evening.

I drifted farther into the room. "So, what are you working on?" I pointed at the maps.

"Oh, we're doing a piece on Communist rebels in the Philippines and—"

"Yeah, good, that sounds good." I reached the desk. "So . . . last night? I went to the bar to see *you*."

Adam's mouth remained a thin line. "Yeah, I could tell by the way you ran in the other direction, arms pinwheeling."

I nodded, once. "Yes. Fair. True. I did do that. It's just . . ." I hesitated. "You seem sort of . . . comically great."

"Like I could be a great comedian?"

"Oh, God, I'm doing this wrong." I hung my head. I was doing it wrong *again*. Seriously, I needed to look into my benefits package and see if my health plan covered this. Maybe I could get behavioral therapy. Like an anger management class, but dating management. Maybe.

"It seemed *promising*," I said helplessly, "and so of course I bungled the whole thing. I do that, you know. I bungle and I ramble, and look, I'm doing it right now as I'm trying to talk about it."

What a mess. But then I looked up. He was smiling. Surprised. And flattered.

And . . . interested?

"You caught me off guard, is what I'm saying." I took a step back, a little intimidated by the directness of his gaze and the undeniable look in his eye. "I mean, why would you like me? With your . . ." Words failed me, and I trailed off.

"My what?" Adam asked.

"You know." I gestured to his hair, his smile, his Yale diploma.

He seemed confused.

I pretended to be rowing.

"Weird swimming?" Adam asked.

I rowed harder.

"Old-timey railroad car?"

"Crew championship!" I shouted, exasperated.

He looked at me like I was nuts. "Wow, I never would have gotten that, seriously. How do you even know about that?"

"There's gossip about *you* around this network too, you know."

"And the juiciest thing they can come up with is my collegiate athletic career? I don't know whether to be relieved or depressed."

"So anyway," I said. "I just didn't think that you *liked* me."

"But I do," Adam said, standing. "Oddly, a lot. You're different. And a deeply terrible mime."

I laughed despite myself.

"I asked you out."

"Kinda."

"I did," he insisted. "And then when I saw you in the bar

I practically tackled you to the ground. What part of that was confusing to you?"

It shouldn't have been. It hadn't been, at first. And then . . . "My radar for that kind of thing is off."

"Guess so."

Maybe I should wear a bracelet, I thought, *like diabetics*. It would warn any potential dates that I was astoundingly slow when it came to these things. "I can't really tell if a man is interested in me unless he's naked."

Adam gaped at me.

"No, you don't have to get naked," I said quickly. Well, unless he *wanted* to. "You know what I mean. It's like the pants come off and I think, *Oh, all right, guess he doesn't actually want to check out my CD collection*."

He laughed. "Wow, you're nuts, huh?"

I sighed. Finally, he *gets* it. "Yes." But then I smiled. "That going to be a problem?"

"Okay, look. Let's start over. Maybe I'm to blame with that whole 'meet some friends at a bar' thing."

"Yes, great idea," I said. "We'll put some blame on you."

"So this time we'll go out to dinner like regular people. Take it slow, see where it leads. Sound good?"

I beamed. "Sounds perfect."

So we had dinner together, which was lovely—some cozy little Italian place Adam knew—and then he took me back to his apartment to, um, check out his CD collection.

Which was also lovely.

I can't tell you who made the first move. It all happened so quickly. But next thing I knew, we were making out like crazy

111

on the couch. And not like I'd report this to Sasha and Tracy tomorrow, but Adam Bennett, on top of being a journalistic scion and a Yale grad and a crew champion and a certified hottie, is also a damned good kisser.

Damned. Good.

Eventually, as the second half of the TV on the Radio album revved up, my shirt came off, and so did his.

"You know," I said. "It's a perfectly nice CD collection."

"Mmmm . . ." Adam nibbled his way along my collarbone. His hands slipped down my torso to fumble with the clasp of my skirt.

"But I should probably start heading home. It's *eight o'clock* already." Damn morning show schedules. How would I ever have a normal social life?

"Yes," he said, as he got the button undone. "You should go. You should go." And then the zip.

"It's Mike's first day tomorrow," I protested between kisses.

"Then definitely," he said, kissing my neck, my shoulders. "Definitely go. Go."

I moaned a little and ran my fingers down his spine. Yeah, I should go home. I should. I should.

I probably should *not* have had that glass of limoncello at the end of the meal. It made me feel so . . . liquid. Adam also tasted like citrus. I wondered if he still rowed regularly. The breadth of his shoulders would indicate he did. Now I understood why he liked to keep his shirt untucked. Draw some attention away from the phenomenal, triangular shape of his . . .

He rolled on top of me, and I totally lost my train of thought.

"You know what?" I gave in. "What's the big whoop?

Mike's done this before. He knows what he's doing." I tightened my grip around him.

"Yeah," said Adam, and then a second later he stopped doing whatever that delicious thing he was doing to my neck. "Um . . ."

"Mmm-hmm?"

He bolstered himself up on his elbows and looked down at me, his face a mix of annoyance and resignation. "He didn't, by chance, open a bottle of forty-year-old Bruichladdich, did he?"

I stared up at him, wide-eyed. "How do you know that?"

He sighed and slid off me, and I got the distinct impression that our evening of fun and games had just come to an unceremonious halt.

"When I was working with him, if there was something he didn't want to do—cover the Olympics or the Oscars or, you know, something people might get a tiny twinge of pleasure from—the night before, he'd go on a bender."

"*What?*" I sat straight up.

"Classic self-sabotage," Adam said. "And it always started with the Bruichladdich. I've fished him out of dives all over the world, looking like Rocky before they cut his eye."

I started breathing hard again, and this time, it had nothing to do with the half-naked man sitting next to me. Okay, okay, okay . . .

I held my breath, then let it out. "No. This is ridiculous. I'm not going to chase him. He wants to screw this up, that's on him."

I cast a glance at Adam, who looked utterly unconvinced by my little speech.

"Damn it," I said under my breath.

Adam sighed again. "Start at Elaine's."

I sprang off the couch and sprinted for the door. The second I hit the hallway, I looked down at my barely covered chest.

"Shit!" I ran back to Adam's. He met me at the door, holding out my blouse.

"Thank you!"

"Oh, please don't," he replied, chagrined. "Don't thank me for ruining our night."

I gave him a quick kiss. "Later."

If I didn't get fired.

11

Elaine's was one of those immortal Manhattan restaurants that natives worshipped and non–New Yorkers knew only if they were deeply into Woody Allen. When I asked directions from the doorman in Adam's apartment, he looked at me like I'd just gotten off the bus. Then again, it might have had something to do with the mussed state of my hair and lipstick.

The bar at Elaine's boasted an impressive population of Who's Who and an even more impressive whiskey list, but no sign of Mike. I tracked down Elaine herself for my next clue.

"Pomeroy?" she said with a wry and disturbingly knowing smile. "He left a few hours ago."

Crap. I was going to kill him for real. In one fell swoop, he'd threatened my (practically pathetic) career *and* my (finally looking up after a generally equally pathetic) love life.

I tried the Algonquin bar up the street. Seems he'd hit that one, too. Ditto Bond 45.

Kill him, kill him, kill him. I didn't know if it was the lighting design in those bars or what, but I'd definitely started seeing red.

At Smith's Bar, a helpful patron related—after I plied him with an overpriced shot of Lagavulin—that Mike had headed toward '21' Club.

This time, I took a taxi. My feet had started developing blisters sometime during the second hour of my search, and I'd slipped off my heels. I could have been in bed with *Adam Bennett* right now. I could have been in my *own* bed, asleep even. I could have been anywhere in the world tonight. Instead, I was tracking down the star of my show before he ruined my entire life.

Honestly, I was surprised they let me through the door at '21'. My hair was a mess, my shirt was buttoned wrong, my feet were bare, and I'm pretty sure my skirt was twisted front to back. But let me in they did.

Maybe they were used to crazy news producers hunting for Mike Pomeroy. Probably never so early in the evening before, though. Welcome to the world of morning news.

And there he was, in the back, entertaining a table of people I was embarrassed to see in my state of dishabille. It was like a Who's Who in Television party. Every single one of them made more in a year than the combined lifetime income of my entire family.

And yet, I marched forward. "Mike," I said.

He turned to me. "Uh-oh. The missus."

I stomped my way, barefoot, to the table, fuming.

An MSNBC luminary grinned at me. "Incoming."

"Jesus, Pomeroy," said a twelve-time Emmy winner from CBS. "They're getting younger and younger."

I reached him and clamped a hand down on his shoulder. "Mike, I need to talk to you." He reeked of the rotting smoky smell of very expensive scotch.

"Why?" Mike said. "Is the baby mine?" He held up a high five to another anchor. "Up top, man."

I shook my head and dragged him out of the chair. It was easy, given how intoxicated he was. The others looked on, surprised.

"Outside," I said. "Now."

But I couldn't wait until we were on the street to start my lecture. I was far too angry. "I'll have you know," I said, seething, "that this show is *very important to a lot of people—* including, but not limited to, *me.*"

A few more patrons turned in our direction.

I almost shoved Mike out the door. He stumbled into the street.

"Don't you get it?" I asked. "This is my *ass* on the line here!"

Mike stopped dead. He spun slowly to face me. "Actually, your ass is irrelevant. You're a footnote. It's *my* ass. My reputation. My integrity. Mine."

I took two steps forward until we were face-to-face. "You are egotistical and selfish."

Mike didn't blink. "I'm *on-air talent.*"

Enough. "All right, let's go."

"Where?" Mike asked.

"Home." I whistled for a cab. Mike flinched and covered his ears.

I directed the cab to take us to Mike's place, and when we

arrived, he practically slammed the taxi door in my face. "Okay," he growled. "I'm home. You can leave."

"No way," I said. I marched up to the front door of his building and waved him inside. "Let's go, Pops."

He trudged after me.

In some ways, Mike's apartment looked pretty much as I'd expected it would. Expensive, in keeping with his multimillion-dollar contract, and masculine—though thankfully he'd declined to hang the walls with the taxidermied remains of his hunting trophies. And yet, there were a few touches that seemed more like the Mike I'd once idolized than of the jackass who'd been showing up to work all week. Beautiful artwork adorned those walls that weren't covered in bookshelves crammed with first editions.

So there was a side of him that wasn't a total troglodyte. Good to know, since he certainly wasn't showing it at the moment, as he blundered his way into the kitchen to pour himself a nightcap. I chose to believe that one more, at this stage, wouldn't hurt him.

I took a stance in front of the door. He stuck his head out of the kitchen, looked at me, and burst out laughing.

"I'm glad you're amused," I replied, stone-cold.

"You're alone tonight," he slurred. "Makes sense. Let me guess. You meet a guy, have"—he waved his scotch glass around—"three dates, and the whole time you have nothing to talk about but your job."

I refused to let any emotion cross my face.

"And he conveniently loses your number."

I blinked, and he got a triumphant gleam in his eyes.

"Yeah," he said, nodding, like he'd just uncovered some great state secret. "So, apart from your obvious father issues—did he leave you? Die?"

I blinked again.

"You've got that repellent 'moxie' going on—"

"Shut up," I said. "Fifteen minutes ago I was a 'footnote.' So why are you suddenly so fascinated by my psychological scars?" I gestured at his apartment, at all the photos and mementos of his life. The souvenirs he'd brought back from trips abroad. The pictures of his family. The framed snapshot of the time he'd gone fishing with the Clintons. "Look at all these stories you could be doing, based on things you're actually interested in. Modern art, hunting and fishing . . ."

I grabbed a photo off an end table. "Is this your grandson? I didn't even know you had grandkids. You could do parenting segments. You could bring your family down to the show and—"

"Those ungrateful shits?" said Mike. "No thank you." He snatched the photo from my hand. "The tour is over, fangirl. Go back to your sad little life. Go away."

"Not on your life." I sat on the couch. "I'm staying right here to make sure you don't bolt again."

Mike shrugged. "Suit yourself. Sleep tight."

"Oh, I'm not going to be sleeping, thanks." I sat ramrod-straight and stared at the wall.

He gripped the photo even tighter in his hands and left the room. So apparently he hated the ungrateful little shit enough to take him into the bedroom? Interesting.

I remained where I was, determined to keep my word. I would stay awake. I would. I needed to be alert enough to wake him up tomorrow, to get him on the air.

"I'm awake," I whispered. "Awake, awake, awake."

Awake . . .

. . .

It was raining outside. The droplets were pattering on the window, behind the lace curtains my mom had hung in the bedroom when I was six years old.

She poked my shoulder.

"Ten more minutes, Mom," I said, and rolled over.

In response, she yanked off my blanket. "Let's go, fangirl."

I opened my eyes. *Fangirl*. I was asleep on Mike's couch.

I sat up. Mike was standing over me in a robe, poking me with some sort of tribal rain stick. I grabbed my BlackBerry. Three A.M. Phew. We were safe.

"You want breakfast?" he said to me, still wielding the rain stick like he was an old lady with a sharp-edged umbrella.

"I . . ." I rubbed my eyes. I wanted to curl up and go back to bed. Or to bed at all. Mike flipped on a light, and I squinted. He looked fabulous, like he'd just come back from a week at a spa. I caught sight of myself in the hall mirror.

Hagsville.

Mascara was smeared beneath my eyes. My hair, through the combined magic of a makeout session with Adam, a frenzied race through the streets of Manhattan, and a night on a leather couch, had all the qualities of a particularly intricate bird's nest. My shirt had seen better days. I was actually *missing* buttons now.

Years from now, would Becky Fuller's only lasting claim to fame be that she once lost buttons in Mike Pomeroy's sofa?

"I'm making breakfast." He vanished into the kitchen.

I dragged myself over to the island and watched him crack eggs into a bowl.

"You ever seen a real egg?" Mike shoved one under my nose. I blinked wearily at it. "This one is from a pastured hen in Maryland. I get them delivered once a week."

"So New York chickens aren't good enough for you?" I asked.

Mike started whisking.

"We have to go," I said.

But he wasn't listening. "Now, the beauty of a frittata is it can be made with any ingredients. Anything you have on hand."

He checked out the contents of his refrigerator, his mood so cheery you'd have thought he'd gotten laid last night. As someone who'd very narrowly—and very regretfully—*missed* getting laid, I remained unamused.

"Come on," I tried again. "Get dressed."

"You want me to starve?" He pulled out a bunch of vegetables. Chanterelles, shallots, tomatoes.

Actually, if I was going to be perfectly honest, it looked pretty good. But I wasn't in the mood for gourmet breakfasts. I was in the mood for a double shot of espresso and an anchorman on my morning show. Stat.

"I need to be in tip-top shape. I'm about to appear on television in front of . . . oh, six people?" He started chopping.

I yawned. "At least eight."

"You're going to love this, I promise." Mike started warming up a pan on the stove.

"Mike," I pleaded. "*Come on.*"

In order to get him to put on his suit and shave, I promised to watch the frittata as it browned in the oven. The scent of sautéed shallots and mushrooms wafted up to me out of the warm oven, but I refused to be tempted. Even though the frittata was certainly enough for two, I would not allow this lunacy to continue. We had donuts at the studio. Mike was just trying to give me a heart attack.

I gave myself five minutes to make myself presentable. I used Mike Pomeroy's mouthwash, scrubbed my face with Mike Pomeroy's soap, and stole one of Mike Pomeroy's shirts.

I found him in the kitchen, the frittata on a plate. "Aren't you done with that yet?"

He placed a finger against the dish. "Still too hot. See, what a lot of people don't know is that the frittata is meant to be eaten at room temperature. It was invented in Italy for the afternoon repast."

I slammed my hands down on the countertop. "Hey, Mike, guess what? I *don't care* about your epicurean breakfast. We're going to be late. *Let's go!*"

And so I dragged the great Mike Pomeroy—kicking and screaming and nibbling on room-temperature frittata—to his first broadcast of *Daybreak*. We were late to the staff meeting, which meant everyone stared as we came in. Mike looked impeccable. I looked like I'd gotten caught in a freak tornado.

Lenny gave me a once-over. "Where have you been?"

"Long story." I sat down beside him and tried to smooth my hair.

Mike ambled over to the empty chair next to Colleen. "She spent the night at my place."

Every last person on the *Daybreak* staff stared in shock. Colleen's jaw dropped.

Mike nodded at her, his expression lascivious. "Morning, Pacoima."

Everyone was still gaping at me. "Oh, come on, people, please. I slept on the couch."

"Until I woke her up with my African rain stick," Mike said brightly.

"African . . . ," began Lenny.

". . . Rain stick?" Colleen finished.

Sasha and Tracy and Lisa and Ernie all goggled.

I leveled dagger eyes at Mike. *Shut up, you ass.* Moving right along. "All right," I said, affecting my best executive producer voice. "Today is Mike's first show. Big day for us. So let's run through the lineup one more time."

I'd gotten Mike here. What he chose to do now was up to him.

After the meeting, I washed up. I was attacking my hair in the ladies' room when I saw in the mirror Colleen standing behind me. She was holding one of her suits.

"Always keep extras," she said. "I've been vomited on by enough octuplets, shat on by enough bald eagles, and had enough blenders filled with summer gazpacho explode on me over the years that I've got an entire second wardrobe in my dressing room."

I took it from her. "Thank you."

"I mean, if your hips fit in there." She gave me a once-over. "You . . . didn't sleep with him, did you?"

I groaned. "No. I chased him all over Manhattan and then stood guard at his door to make sure he didn't ditch us at the last minute. I care about the *show*. That's all."

She regarded me for a long moment. "I know," she said at last. "That's why you get the suit." And then she left.

I changed into Colleen's suit and decided, in a fit of kindness, not to tell her the skirt was big on me. I finished putting myself back together, dabbed in vain at the dark, baggy circles under my eyes, and gave myself one last pep talk.

Becky Fuller, you are the executive producer of Daybreak, *a national morning show. You have landed yourself a cohost who is one of the greatest television news reporters of all time. And, against all odds, he'll be premiering on the show this morning. You did it.*

And just as I was starting to feel pretty good, my head decided to stick in a caveat:

But don't celebrate yet. He could still fuck it all up. And he might do so just out of spite.

I sighed. Given Mike's attitude this morning, it made sense to prepare myself for the worst. Still, we had several things going for us. Mike Pomeroy, possibly because very few people on earth realized what a jerk he was, had one of the highest Q ratings of any broadcaster on the network. Women loved the mix of his distinguished, silver-haired air and the wicked charmer glint in his eye, and the reaction to our promo spots had been overwhelmingly positive, especially among the largely untapped male market. Maybe we'd be the morning show that got the guys watching. Maybe they'd switch from CNN or MSNBC and check out *Daybreak.* Wouldn't Jerry be pleased if I pulled off *that* little coup?

I strode into the control room, chin up and finally feeling more human in Colleen's borrowed suit. Lenny and a few of the other producers were checking the monitors to make sure we hadn't missed any late-breaking news.

"What are they promoting on the *Today* show this morning?" I asked.

He snorted. Was that a good snort or a bad snort? I looked at the screen.

Oh, no. Vieira had scored an interview with the drunk-driving Playboy Playmate. As the *Today* log flashed on the monitor, a cheery voice-over read, "She ran over Hef's dog . . . then buried it near the Jacuzzi. Hear all the details, today on *Today.*"

The scene changed to shots of the Playmate in the April

124

spread. She smiled coyly at the camera while the most interesting parts of her nude body were blacked out. So much for getting the male viewership.

"You're kidding me," I said to Lenny.

"Oh," he replied. "It gets worse." He pointed to another monitor, "Check out *Good Morning America*."

I covered my eyes with my fingers. "Do I really want to?"

"Sawyer's doing Clooney."

I dropped my hands. "That *bitch*." Another silver-haired charmer. We were finished.

12

Tension seemed strung across the set along with the lighting and camera cables. The tech crew was unusually quiet, the hands of the makeup artist trembled a bit as she reapplied Colleen's blusher, and I was glad I hadn't taken Mike up on his offer of frittata, as I was pretty sure I'd have spewed egg, chanterelles, and shallots all over the set.

Mike and Colleen sat at the anchor desk, hair perfectly groomed, outfits coordinated and spotless. I watched them in the frame on the monitors. "They look good together," I said to Lenny. "At least we have that going for us."

Lenny nodded, then crossed himself.

"Great," I said. "The Jewish guy is crossing himself. Glad we're feeling so confident." I turned back to the monitor. "Come on, Pomeroy," I said under my breath.

The *Daybreak* intro began. The monitors showed the taped intro, the new one we'd done, with shots of Mike and

Colleen smiling at each other over the news desk, Mike running up the steps to the courthouse—artfully cropped so he had nothing to complain about—old shots of Colleen petting the trunk of a baby elephant, and smiling with Britney Spears on the plaza, plus one of Mike shaking hands with the Dalai Lama that I'd dug up in the archives.

On the set, I saw Colleen turn to Mike. "Don't bore the nation into a coma with your dull news crap, okay?"

Mike pretended to be very interested in his notes. "Yes. Certainly." He raised his head and smiled at her. "Oh, and suck it."

The *Daybreak* logo sparkled across the screen as an announcer finished his voice-over detailing the day's schedule. "Those stories and more this morning on *Daybreak* with your hosts, live from New York City, Colleen Peck . . . and Mike Pomeroy."

"Good morning, everyone." Colleen's smile could have put a head cheerleader to shame. "Before we begin, today is a historic moment here on *Daybreak*: the day that Mike Pomeroy joins our little show."

Okay, the "very special episode" tone in her voice was a tad saccharine, but with any luck, it was only temporary. She turned to Mike, smile still firmly affixed. That's my girl. Colleen. Such a pro.

"We are lucky to have a journalist of your caliber here. Welcome."

"Yes" was all Mike said.

Her smile faltered. I knew her well enough to know what she was thinking under that perfect coif. *Are you fucking kidding me?* And I was feeling exactly the same way.

But she soldiered on. "And to commemorate your first day, we have a little surprise for you!"

Come on, Mike. Be a good sport. Be a good sport. I'd wanted to nix this part, but apparently, it was a *Daybreak* tradition. I'd even argued on the side of superstition, saying that maybe doing this every time was what was cursing our male anchors. I was overruled. And in the interest of staff morale, I let it go through.

But judging by the way Mike was resolutely ignoring the techs as they wheeled out a gigantic cake emblazoned with WELCOME MIKE in icing letters a foot high, I now realized that they—and I—might live to regret that decision.

Colleen clasped her hands together. "Happy *first* day to you," she sang, "Happy *first* day to you . . ."

Mike's eyes widened a fraction, and then, as if nothing had happened, he turned to the monitors. "Thank you."

Should I have been happy we'd at least gotten two syllables out of him this time?

"Now, onto today's top stories," said Mike. "In Texas today, severe weather continues to plague the Gulf Coast. . . ."

Lenny looked at me. "So far, he's a warm fuzzy blanket."

I rolled my eyes. So much for being a good sport.

Behind me, Merv, the *Daybreak* director, was calling the shots as we went from story to story with far more speed than we'd expected. There was zero banter. When Mike reported elevated levels of geothermal activity in Yellowstone Park, Colleen opened her mouth, but he plowed ahead into a discussion of scientists' predictions of the likelihood of a supervolcano. When he reported the results of the election in France, she made half a joke about croissants, and he changed the subject to the situation in Guam.

I waved at Mike and gave him a slow-down motion. He ignored me. I tried to mime "banter"—clutching my stomach and pretending to laugh.

While the shot was on Colleen, Mike gave me a quizzical glance.

Adam was right. I was a truly terrible mime. Maybe I needed to learn sign language. Or whatever motions referees use.

"Now to Ernie Appleby with the weather," Colleen said.

Ernie's Q ratings, I'd been pleased to see, were stratospheric. He was quite possibly the cheeriest weatherman on television. Such was people's love for his unwavering good cheer that their approval was maintained even when he was completely off base on the forecast.

Which was disappointingly often. Still, don't mess with it if it ain't broken. Our public liked to see him on TV, even if he had no idea how to predict the weather. It was the type of attitude that no doubt gave Mike hives, but I didn't care. Ernie was solid.

"Thanks, Colleen." He bubbled over with warmth. "I'd like to take a moment to welcome Mike Pomeroy to his first broadcast. As one hurricane said to another, 'I have my eye on you.'"

I'm sure his fans were smiling. Mike's face might have been one of those Easter Island stone heads.

But Ernie didn't seem to notice the lack of reception from the anchor. "Looking across the country this morning," he said, gesturing to the green screen behind him, "you'll see low-pressure systems in the Midwest bringing in that wet weather. . . ."

As Ernie continued his broadcast, I made a few more desperate attempts to get Mike's attention. I waved my arms. I jumped up and down. I considered flashing the lights in the control booth. He ignored me.

On the set, but offscreen, Colleen turned to him, peeved.

He might snub her, but no one snubbed Ernie the weatherman.

"It's the morning," she said. "Not a funeral. Crack a smile, Mount Rushbore."

"Cram it, Methuselah," came Mike's reply.

Okay, that was it. I ran out onstage, wearing a fake smile that might have given even Colleen's a run for its money, Maybe it was her suit that had this effect on me, but even my voice came out merrier than I'd expected.

"Guys," I said, "I was wondering if we could take the energy up a notch."

Mike just stared at me.

Colleen clucked her tongue. "I get any more energetic and I'll fly right out of my seat."

"*You're* doing great," I said to Colleen. We both glared pointedly at Mike.

"Out of my way," he said. "Camera's back in three."

I trudged back to the control room. Lenny handed me my coffee mug. "Do you need something stronger in there?" he asked.

I set my jaw. "They're just getting warmed up."

Fortunately, the next story was a bit of hard news, so Mike was right in his element. The camera ate him up: the intensity in his eyes, the cadence of his gravelly, commanding voice. Every staff member on set leaned in, soaking up his report.

". . . He apparently works alone," Mike was telling the camera, "gaining access to homes through unlocked windows and doors."

At my side in the control room, Merv signaled for a police sketch to pop up on-screen. Even in pencil, the guy looked like a creep. The words "Sexual Predator at Large" flashed on the chyron at the bottom of the screen as Mike finished his report.

"Local police in Milwaukee are asking anyone who recognizes this sketch to contact them immediately."

I smiled at Lenny in triumph. There. A thing of beauty.

"In other news," Mike said after a beat, "former president Jimmy Carter continued his campaign for human rights in Beijing this week."

Merv switched over to a picture of Carter.

"He's meeting with political protesters and calling for a renewed dialogue between—"

I glanced at the monitor. The words "Sexual Predator at Large" still graced the chyron.

Yikes. "Lenny!" I hissed.

Lenny was enthralled by Mike's newscast.

"Merv!" I hissed louder.

Ditto.

I lunged for the control panel and wiped the chyron.

"Guys, Jesus!" I said, collapsing in the nearest chair. Were we going to get calls about that one. Lots of calls. Calls from Jerry, maybe.

Lenny looked down at me and shook his head. "I'm getting the bourbon."

I was too stunned to respond.

"Becky—"

"At least . . . ," I began weakly. "At least it can't get any worse?"

On set, Colleen beamed at the camera. Mike gave the audience his patented superserious anchorman face. They looked like theater masks of comedy and tragedy.

I buried my head in my hands.

Lenny brought me bourbon-laced coffee, which I ignored. The broadcast went on.

"Tomorrow on *Daybreak*," I heard Colleen say with a note of false cheer, "we'll show you eight things you *didn't* know you could do with potatoes. Ooh, that should be fun."

"Also," Mike boomed, "we'll talk to some relief workers who say the international community has abrogated their duty to protect victims of natural disasters around the world."

I lifted my head and stared numbly at the set.

"And," he went on, "that their cries for help have proven bootless."

Colleen blinked at the screen for a moment, then did her best to compensate. "And . . . after that, what your toothbrush says about *you*!"

I turned to Lenny, in physical pain. "Did he just say 'abrogate'?"

He nodded. "Also 'bootless.'"

I'd started to hyperventilate, so I grabbed the mug and slammed back some lukewarm coffee-with-whiskey. "I think I just exited my body."

"That might be a good strategy," said Lenny, watching the train wreck continue.

At long last, Colleen, her smile certainly frayed around the edges, addressed the camera one last time. "And that's our show this morning. Welcome to the *Daybreak* family, Mike, and thank you for—"

"Thank you, everyone," Mike cut in. "Goodbye."

I caught my breath. At least it was finally over.

Colleen pursed her lips. "Goodbye."

Mike gave a little nod to the screen. "Goodbye."

Colleen cast him a quick, pissed glare. "Good*bye*."

"How many is that?" I asked Lenny.

"Two each." Lenny's hangdog expression was more miserable than usual.

"Oh, dear Jesus," I said.

"Amen," said Lenny, and he crossed himself again. If this kept up, I was writing a letter of concern to his rabbi.

On set, they were still going at it.

"Bye," said Colleen.

"Bye," said Mike.

"*Bye,*" said Colleen.

"*BYE,*" said Mike.

"And we're out!" I cried, and cut the feed.

In the control room, we all stood in shell-shocked silence. The houselights went up on the set. Mike straightened his tie, stood, and walked offstage, whistling.

I knew that Colleen, however, might need physical restraints to keep her from committing homicide right there in the studio. As I exited the control room, she pointed a finger at me. "Gidget," she said. "You get that asshole in line, or I'm going to walk."

"I'll talk to him," I said, holding up my hands. She wouldn't walk. She couldn't. She was still the face of *Daybreak*, which meant she needed us as much as we needed her. We needed her consistency, and the small but solid fan base she brought to the show. (Not to mention how easy she was on our budget.) And she needed the show. The best Colleen could hope for outside of us was heading back to local news in Arizona, and I doubted she wanted to leave Manhattan.

"All you've been *doing* is talking to him," said Colleen. "That and playing nursemaid on his couch. It's obviously not making a difference."

"I know, I know." I shook my head. "But I'll try again."

"I'm sick of hearing that," said Colleen. "And of knowing

that it won't make a difference. *This* was unacceptable. I was giving it my all, and Mike was making a mockery of the whole thing."

"I know," I repeated, flapping my hands in the hope she'd keep her rant to a dull roar. "We all know that we can't have a repeat of this show. We have some kinks to work out."

"He has no respect at all for our format," she said. "He wouldn't even give an inch."

"Colleen," I said, exasperated. "Do you somehow think I wasn't right here watching every second of what just happened? You're preaching to the choir. And there's nothing else for me to do except to promise you that in a few seconds, I am going to go see Mike and work this out."

She regarded me for a long moment. "Oh, I believe you'll go see Mike," she said. "I'm just doubtful you can budge him."

I glowered at her; she gave it right back. I stood there, in Colleen's borrowed suit, and swore to myself that I'd never give her, or anyone else on this set, a reason to doubt me again.

And I swore that Mike Pomeroy had better watch out.

13

By the time I got to Mike's dressing room, he was gone. And he wasn't at Craft Services or in the men's room—I checked. He hadn't gone to the other floors or the archives, or to Elaine's for a ridiculously early drink.

I finally tracked him down at a shoe-shine stand near the IBS building.

When he saw me, he gave me the most expectant, innocent look a human could muster. I wanted to throttle him, but the shoe guy would have been witness to my crime.

"May I help you?"

I launched into him without preamble. "You said you would banter."

"No." He lifted a finger in protest. "*You* said I would banter."

"And you agreed! I distinctly recall you saying that you'd do it once you were on air."

"I said I would talk about the headlines," he corrected. "And I did."

"Barely!"

"I said I would anchor a news show. That's what my contract calls for. That's what I'm going to do."

And here I'd gotten the man *mangoes*. "Mike," I said. "You can't just go out there and give monosyllabic answers and talk about natural disasters."

"You sure about that, fangirl? 'Cause I think I just did."

"Colleen had to carry the entire show."

I tried appealing to his vanity. "Is that really what you want? The media saying stuff about how you're a sidekick to Colleen Peck?"

For a second, he almost seemed to listen. But then the placid smile was back. "I think you sealed my reputation the second you forced me onto your insipid show, don't you?"

I choked on all the words I wanted to say to him.

"Anyway," he continued, "what are you doing here? You need to go back to your office and wait for the phone call from Jimmy Carter. You know: Jimmy Carter, 'Sexual Predator.'"

He actually made air quotes. My hands tightened into fists at my sides.

"Now, go away. I'm busy." He waved me off and returned to checking the headlines on his cell.

The shoe guy gave me a sympathetic shrug.

I walked away as quickly as I could, eyes and throat both burning.

Somehow, I made it through the rest of the day. The call from Jimmy Carter's people was actually not so bad. They hadn't seen the show themselves—natch—and were merely responding to reports about what had happened. And, you know, the YouTube video, which I notified Legal to have zapped as soon as possible. Legal, in turn, warned me that any zappage would be of course temporary, and that probably the best fix for the whole matter was to make sure the writers on IBS's nightly talk show included a joke about it to diffuse the situation.

Much harder to stomach were the phone calls from the elderly audience of *Daybreak* who'd been appalled, frankly *appalled*, to see our thirty-ninth president falsely vilified on our show. We put up a correction on the IBS website and promised to run another one at the beginning of tomorrow's show.

I had a stern talking-to with the entire staff about paying attention to chyrons.

Lenny offered to take the blame for the mishap and tender his resignation. I told him if he left, I'd have a nervous breakdown, and to pass the bourbon.

Colleen had already gone home for the day. To be honest, I was relieved. I didn't see any way of facing her after she'd so accurately predicted the outcome of my conversation with Mike.

I had no way of controlling my on-air talent. My last-ditch effort to save this show had been an utter miscalculation. I wasn't sure if I could save *Daybreak* now. Maybe what they'd said was right about me: Maybe I wasn't qualified for this job. Maybe I would fail, just as Colleen had predicted. Maybe they had been right, back at *Good Morning, New Jersey*, to pick blue-chip Chip instead of blue-plate me. All this time, I'd thought if I could just stick with it a little longer, just show them exactly what I could do, I could make it happen.

Well, I showed them. And what ended up happening was

a disastrous show in which I managed to call a former leader of the free world a rapist.

Later, after I sent most of the staff home early, I sat in my office and waited around for Jerry's call. Couldn't wait to hear his take on the situation. Maybe he'd tell me that if I'd bothered to take a few more broadcasting courses, I'd know how to work something as simple as a chyron graphic. Maybe he'd tell me that he would have thought someone in the role of executive producer would be able to manage her staff better. Maybe he would gloat over how he'd warned me about hiring Mike Pomeroy.

Or maybe he'd skip all that for something short and sweet like: *You're fired.*

But Jerry didn't call, and as I sat there, staring at the phone and waiting for the summons that would seal my doom, I began to wonder why it was that he wasn't calling. I mean, I'd half expected him to ring even if the show had gone well. After all, I'd just debuted Mike Pomeroy on morning television.

Maybe he'd slept through it all? But even if he had, surely he'd heard about it. If IBS Legal knew about the Carter situation, Jerry must have heard. Right?

After another half an hour of fretting, I realized there was no way I'd make it if I just sat and waited for the ax to fall. So I picked up the phone and called Jerry's office.

His secretary told me he'd been out today.

He still had to have heard about our screwup. Which meant he didn't even think we were important enough to deal with right away. Fabulous.

No point me sitting around here. It was obvious that no one, from our host to our executives to the guy responsible for wiping the damn chyrons, gave a shit about the show. What was I doing spending the entire night in my office?

There were surely better things to be doing. I could think of at least one.

Adam answered the door as soon as I knocked. It was a risk, coming to his place unannounced. I knew that. He might not be home. Or worse, he might be home, but entertaining some blond regatta-attending goddess. That would really cap the evening off.

But instead he was standing there, looking at me, dressed in a pair of jeans and a faded Yale T-shirt.

"Did you see it?" I asked miserably.

He looked at Colleen's too-big suit. "It wasn't that bad. It—"

Adam had watched the show! I threw myself into his arms and kissed him.

"Uh, hi." He backed us both into his apartment and kicked the door shut.

"You know what?" I said. "On second thought, I *don't* want to talk about it." I kissed him again.

"Sounds like a plan," Adam murmured.

We stumbled into his apartment, still locked at the lips, and I reflected on how high my Manhattan rent was and how ridiculously long it had been since I'd been in my own shoebox of an apartment. Adam, it seemed, had better taste in real estate than I. Or possibly more money to burn on rent. Maybe both, come to think of it. At any rate, his place boasted an actual view. It was of the street beyond and a glimpse of skyline, but it was still much nicer than my brick wall and alleyway.

"Last night . . . ," I began, as he was nibbling on my neck.

"Yeah?"

"I didn't get a chance to tell you how much I like your place."

"Oh." He started fumbling with the buttons on my top. "Well, you're free to admire it as much as you want now. Shall we start the tour with the bedroom?"

"Awfully confident, aren't you?"

He grinned at me. "You just tackled me at the front door. I didn't think you dropped by for a game of Scrabble."

"True." I slid my hands underneath his tee. He did the same under Colleen's blazer.

My BlackBerry began buzzing in my pocket. We both froze, but when I started to pull away, he tightened one hand on my waist, then reached the other into my pocket.

"I should probably take that."

He held it away from me. "Waiting on any life-and-death sources?"

"Um . . ."

"How about relatives in the hospital?"

"No, but—"

"And I assume you already talked to Jimmy Carter?"

"Not as such, but I did speak to—" I lunged for it, but Adam was way taller.

"If it's Pomeroy calling to apologize, I say make the bastard wait." Adam strode over to his fridge and tossed the Black-Berry inside.

"Adam!" I cried.

"We've been interrupted twice now," he said, drawing me back into his arms. "That's plenty at this stage of the game."

"But what if something happens?" I looked over his shoulder at the stainless steel box currently chilling my phone.

"Then you'll miss it." He went back to the buttons on my shirt. "And then someone else will cover the World's Biggest Pumpkin."

"See, that's not fair," I said, helping him slide first Colleen's blazer, then Colleen's blouse, off my shoulders. "You work at a magazine show. You do one fifteen-minute story every two months."

"Oh boy," Adam said, and swept me off my feet. "Here you go again."

But I wasn't done protesting my point, even as he carried me toward his bedroom. "We're doing fifteen stories a day, none more than three minutes."

"Watch your head," he said, as we crossed the threshold.

I ducked to avoid the doorjamb. "Three and a half if it's the president or if there are nude photos. Four if we have both."

"Is that your follow-up to the Carter revelation?"

I gave him a playful smack as he deposited me on his bed. "Watch it, buddy."

"I told you," said Adam. He landed on top of me. "I did. I got up at six A.M. and I watched your show." He took off his shirt. My mouth went dry.

"What, you saying I owe you now?" I unhooked my bra.

He rolled on top of me, grinning. "Whatever works."

"Mmm . . ." Except, before we got too involved, there was one thing I absolutely had to know. "Hey, Adam?"

"Yeah?" His jeans hit the floor.

"How reliable is your alarm clock?"

Much, much later, when I was scrubbed clean and dressed in one of my sharpest suits, I still couldn't shake off the glow of the previous night. Yesterday might have begun disastrously, but Adam had provided a very sweet finish to the day.

I sat in the control room, trying to keep my focus on the show—such as it was, since Mike hadn't loosened up any from yesterday. But at least we weren't delivering insults to world leaders today.

Except I couldn't seem to keep my mind off the soft kiss Adam had given me just before I stole out of his bed in the wee hours and practically skipped home—learning something about New York City as I did so. The whole "City That Never Sleeps" thing is a lie. When you're out in the middle of the night, the streets are silent and empty. No one's around to witness the undeniable bounce in your step after you leave the apartment of your brand-new lover and float home on a delicious cloud of memories from the night before.

"Hey," whispered Lenny. "What's going on with you this morning?"

"Huh?" I snapped out of my reverie. "I mean, nothing."

He smirked. "Surrrre."

"Oh, you're nuts," I said, not quite meeting his eyes. "It's just been a long night."

"Due to . . . ?"

I filtered through the breaking news stories I'd scrambled to get coverage for when I'd finally left Adam's place. There was the new fire out West, the one they were blaming on the work of a serial arsonist. "I put together that whole piece on the arsonist. . . ."

"Riiiiight. That took what? Half an hour?"

I fixed him with a look. "Leave me alone."

"Fine." He held up his hands in surrender.

Just then, one of the producers, Dave, came in, a worried look plastered on his face.

"*Good Morning America* got the mother of the arsonist," he announced.

I shot out of my seat. "Oh, *ass*! I didn't even think of that. Well, I didn't even hear about the whole thing until two A.M.—"

Lenny gave me a look, his suspicions aroused anew.

"All right," I said. "Let's see if the arsonist has a girlfriend. Damn it. Let's see quickly. We only have footage and commentary. . . ."

They stood there for a second.

"Guys," I said, snapping my fingers. "Story. Make it happen."

"But, we're supposed to be doing the thing on garden tools—," Sasha said.

"Arsonist," I said firmly. It was a story I was sure Mike Pomeroy could get behind.

Unfortunately, the arsonist was a loner, his dad was nowhere to be found, and his college roommate was booked on *Today*. Drat. We'd been scooped.

The realization took some of the bloom out of my cheeks, but I wasn't done in yet. My copy was good, the arson expert I'd dug up had solid credentials, we'd gotten some great footage of the fire and the damage, and I had Mike Pomeroy doing the interview. He was ten times more interesting than some guy who hadn't seen his college roommate since he'd dropped out freshman year.

The mother, of course, was going to beat us both.

"It's a sad statement on humanity," Mike said as we walked together toward our lunch meeting, "that the public is more interested in rubbernecking the woman who 'created the monster' than in trying to understand the pathology or the devastation it caused."

"I'm with you there," I said. "But people want to be reassured that their own little tyke won't grow it up to do something like this. They want to look the mom in the eyes and wonder what it is she did wrong."

"Apparently nothing," said Mike. "She didn't have any baby pictures of him playing with matches. They just wanted to watch her cry on national television. And the bozos over at *Good Morning America* were more than happy to milk that for all it's worth." He sneered. "And you wonder why I have no respect for your vaunted *bantering*."

"Okay," I said as we turned the corner. "Forget bantering. I'm taking you out today because I thought we could talk about maybe doing a profile. We're doing a piece on Daniel Boulud—"

"Does it end with me in the kitchen making profiteroles?" Mike asked dryly.

"No."

He gave me a look.

"Braised lamb?" I offered.

He turned and kept walking.

"Okay," I said. "Forget that. How about an interview with Tim McGraw and Faith Hill?"

"If either one becomes president or cures cancer, let me know."

"Mike," I begged.

He stopped for a moment and folded his arms. "I hear you're dating Señor Dipshit. How'd you make that happen?"

I frowned and quickly scanned the area for IBS employees. "Who told you that?" News certainly traveled fast in the office.

"You and him—really?" Mike looked disconcertingly baffled by the notion.

"Um, well, we're not exactly—"

"Because he usually goes out with the girls who are . . ." He stretched his hands apart vertically. "And have . . ." His hands undulated around his torso.

Wow, he was as bad at miming as me.

I cocked my head to the side and tried to decipher. "Taffy pullers with meatballs?"

"You know what I mean."

"Yes," I replied. "But guess what, Mike. I'm not taking the bait."

"Hmph." He kept walking.

"And we're going to talk later about how it's not nice to call people names."

Mike snorted again.

"Because I can think of a few choice ones for you."

"Back atcha, fangirl."

I sighed. One more block. "How about Sean Combs?" I tried. My goal for the day was to nail Mike down with one fluff piece. Just one. If I had to ply him with scotch to get it done, so be it.

"I might," said Mike, "if I knew who that was. But hey, I do have one promising lead. There's an interesting story out of Albany. The governor's tax returns are being audited and—"

"Oh for God's sake!" I cried. This was worse than Ernie and the weather vanes. "You're killing me, Mike. No. No."

"That's a perfectly good story," Mike insisted. For a second, I thought he might stamp his foot. "Could be a great story, in fact. You just don't like it because it doesn't have Britney Spears in it."

"Tell you what," I said. "You get Britney and the governor together, we've got a deal."

He huffed off.

"What wrong with a little human interest? I want the viewers to get to know you."

"And they are supposed to get to know me by seeing me act utterly indifferent to their favorite celebrities?"

"Mike—"

"What you want," he said coldly, "is for me to pander to an audience so you can sell them erectile dysfunction medication. And I won't do that."

I slumped. We'd just turned to walk into the restaurant, with me having my doubts that there was anything I could offer him that would sweeten the pot, when suddenly a woman pounced on us.

"Oh my God!" she shrieked. "It's you! You're that guy!"

Mike took a step or two back from his raving fan. The woman was in her fifties—right in our viewership range—and was dressed in a pair of slacks and a sweater set.

"I just saw you this morning!" she went on, her voice getting well into squeal territory. "I was watching the *Today* show—"

Mike grimaced. "I'm not on—"

"And there was a commercial. So I clicked around, and there you were! Everyone was eating stuffed zucchini and you were all cranky about it and I was like—oh my God, there's that *guy*. You used to do news, right? Like a while ago?"

Used to? Uh-oh. Thanks a bunch, lady. Now I'd never get him on board.

She put her arms around him and held her phone at arm's length, smiling broadly. Mike stood stock still.

"Please remove your hands from my person," he stated.

I heard the phone click, then the fan checked out the results and squealed again. "Oh, this is so great. Thank you!"

"You're welcome," I said, since it was clear Mike would not.

"Dan Rather!" she exclaimed. "I can't believe it."

I clapped my hands to my mouth. Oops.

Mike's face was a thundercloud. He yanked open the door of the restaurant and dashed in.

Okay. Okay, but this really just proved my point. I trailed after him, readying my arguments.

"Mike, you see that—people want to like you."

"No, they want to like Dan Rather."

"They'd know it was you if you put *yourself* out there a little more. You don't need to be so dry on morning television. They want to like you. They want to *know* you. You're in their house every morning, while they're eating breakfast. You're chatting with them. About current events, about the world they live in . . . It's an honor, don't you see that?"

He didn't see. Not at all.

"Mike," I said, defeated. "Can't you just do a few more stories that people will *enjoy*? We're in trouble. I'm in trouble. Help me, *please*."

The hostess eyed us both, her expression alarmed. "Um, table for two?"

14

So, no big surprise, I didn't get through to Mike at all during our lunch. He shot down every one of my story ideas and complained about the public's lowest-common-denominator tastes. At this point, I figured, the only story we might agree on would be getting an interview with the actual arsonist. Doubtless I'd have lots of luck with that one.

As the week wore on, it became clear that my problems were not a product of first-day jitters, but of a genuine miscalculation about the show's capabilities. Perhaps it was time to face facts. I might be a great news producer, but I didn't have the training or experience necessary for a job like this. Sure, I'd had a Rolodex full of useful contacts in Jersey, but that was local news. It took people years to drum up those contacts on the national level. Adam had been in national news his entire career—with a college degree—and he hadn't yet attained executive producer level. Granted, he was at a far more successful show, but still. There was a process to these things.

I could bluff about "Dempsey's people" and "arsonists' girl-friends" as much as I wanted, but in reality, all I had was a very convincing "fake it till you make it" act. I didn't have any real pull.

And neither did anyone else at *Daybreak*—except Mike, and he would back only the stories he wanted. Stories that usually weren't morning show material.

That afternoon, as I watched them tape Lisa's entertainment segment for the following day, I was feeling especially relieved that Mike had taken off. I'd never hear the end of it if he was privy to what was happening on set right now.

I wondered if there was a way to distract him while we played the tape tomorrow.

"Many actors," Lisa was saying, "have changed their names in order to be taken more seriously."

It was a wonder that anyone could take Lisa seriously. Her tan was practically orange, her mouth looked like she was wearing a pair of wax candy lips, and her halter top strained over the overinflated water balloons that passed for her breasts.

Was it possible they'd gotten even bigger recently?

"For instance," she said, "Ricky Schroder became Rick Schroder. The Rock became Dwayne Johnson."

One of the cameramen covered his mouth to hold in his snicker.

Oh, God. Hadn't anyone vetted her copy?

"And Portia de Rossi's name used to be Amanda, but she changed it so as to sound more like the car, which she felt sounded more impressorial."

I turned to Lenny. "*Impressorial?* Are you *sure* I can't fire her?"

He shook his head no.

"What?" I asked. "Is she sleeping with someone?"

Lenny pointed up.

"Jerry?" I said. "Ouch."

A moment later, an intern entered with a message for me from Jerry. Speak of the devil. I took a deep breath. Time to face the music.

"Be right back," I said to Lenny.

Or maybe not.

I was ushered into Jerry's office right away. He kept me standing this time, waiting, while he studied a sheet of ratings.

"Have you seen these?" he said without looking up.

Uh-oh. And here I thought I was just going to be forced to answer for Jimmy Carter. I had to think fast. "Okay, yes, but—"

"You're here to make the ratings worse?" He slammed the paper to his desk. "That's why you came here?"

No, I'd come to make the show better. But I doubted that argument would fly at the moment.

"Thing is," I said, "Mike's still getting up to speed on our format. We're still working on some elements of the show. . . ."

"Getting up to speed?" Jerry scoffed. "You're circling the drain. You rarely book anybody decent because of the ratings, you're not getting any of the big interviews—"

What was the point of denying that? "We just need a little more time . . . ," I said weakly. "I really feel that once Mike has settled into his role we're going to see some big jumps, both in quality and in viewership. The two go hand in hand, I think. With just a touch more patience . . ."

A look of pity crossed Jerry's features. "God, you're even more naïve than I thought."

My brow furrowed. What the hell was he talking about?

He sighed and pushed his chair back. "You have no idea why you have this job, do you?"

"Excuse me?" I asked as he came around and leaned against the front of his desk. The look on his face was the same one my dad had given me when he'd told me the truth about Santa Claus. I began to get the distinct impression that Jimmy Carter's people were the least of my worries.

"It never crossed your mind? Why the network wouldn't give me money to hire a real executive producer?"

Uh, well, things were tight all over. And people didn't want to back . . . oh, shit. A losing horse.

"The network wants to cancel the show," Jerry said.

My heart dropped—not into my stomach. Into something far more painful. Maybe my spleen? My kidneys?

"They want to run game shows and syndicated talk instead. That's why they gave me no budget for an EP. They wanted me to hire someone inept, someone who would run the show into the ground."

"I was someone . . ." I felt faint.

"That way," he explained, "they would feel justified canceling such a long-running show."

"I don't get it," I cried, my tone just shy of frantic. "You're saying you *hired* me . . ." I plopped down on his guest chair. ". . . That you hired *me* to . . . run the show into the ground?"

"No," Jerry said, though his tone was flat. "At first, I figured they'd have it their way, that I'd never find anyone decent enough to save the show. But then you stumbled in here, and for a second, I thought you might have a shot. Especially when you got Pomeroy."

For a moment, my hopes lifted, ever so slightly. So he did think I could do it. And that's why he let me get Mike. Because I was right: It would work. It would be great. Or would have been.

"But the joke's on me, because it turns out you've failed even more completely than the network could have hoped."

Never mind.

"In six weeks," he announced, "they're canceling the show."

"No!"

But Jerry didn't even register my dissent. "So not only will you have significantly weakened our news division, you'll have presided over the demise of a show that's been on the air for forty-seven years."

My heart decided that my spleen hadn't had enough trauma for the day and started sucker-punching it.

"Nice work," Jerry said. "Why don't you go over to PBS and see if you can kill *Sesame Street*."

Oh, God, no. This was far worse than I'd feared. I figured it would be me who was getting fired. That I could handle. That I was used to. After all, I'd already done it once this year. But to be responsible for everyone else losing their jobs? Colleen? Lenny? Sasha, Tracy, Dave . . . oh God: *Ernie*?

Mike would still have his contract. And Lisa would no doubt land on her feet. Merv, our director, could probably get squeezed into another department, but . . .

I'd ruined us all. Because I couldn't hold my show together. Because I couldn't get my anchorman in line. Because I thought it would be a great idea to fire the old host in a fit of "Who's the Boss?" and then hire an unrepentant, curmudgeonly diva in his place.

"Go." Jerry pointed at the door. "You've wasted enough of my time."

I hung my head. Go? Go down and tell them what I'd done? Go down and explain to Lenny that his kids' college funds might be in serious danger? Tell Colleen that she'd been right about me all the time, and that she should probably phone up her friends back in Phoenix? Look directly at Mike as I informed the staff that the show's days were numbered, all because I was as incompetent as the network executives hoped I would be?

I couldn't. I just couldn't.

Finally, I managed to lift my face and look Jerry in the eye. "Can you . . . will you do one thing for me?"

"What?"

"We have six weeks, right?" I asked quickly. "Just don't tell anyone yet. Morale's not exactly at peak to begin with, so . . ."

"Fine." Jerry returned to his desk. "Tell them whenever you want to. It doesn't really matter, does it?"

I left his office. I left his floor. My path through the twisted corridors of the *Daybreak* basement was trod as if I was a member of the walking dead. What was I going to do? What was I going to do?

I turned a corner and ran smack into Lisa.

"There you are!" She bounced. Certain parts of her body bounced a half beat off. "I have a great idea for a segment. Get ready for this!" She paused dramatically and flung out her arms. "Past. Lives."

I blinked.

She nodded at me, her pillow lips parted in excitement. "Like, if we could find out *who* celebrities had been in their previous lives, I think that would be terrific, don't you? Like, what if Justin Timberlake had been Abraham Lincoln?"

I could think of a million responses to this idea. But none of them were worth saying. She could decide that Fergie had been Joan of Arc and report that on *Daybreak* if she wanted. Wouldn't make a difference now.

"Could be very evocatative!" Lisa called after me as I trudged on.

Adam called that night, but I told him I wasn't feeling well. Which was true. I changed into pajama pants and my now-faded I ACCEPT! T-shirt and turned out all the lights. I lay curled up in my bed in my horrible, too-small apartment, and watched the brick wall outside my window. This was the apartment I'd gotten when I thought I had a network career ahead of me. I didn't care how bad it was—job or apartment—because both were just the start of something bigger.

The tough part about wrapping your whole life around something—anything—is that when that thing disappears, you've got nothing left to hold you up. My mother had discovered that when my dad died. Our home was never the same. She'd never intended to support me on her own. She didn't know how to move forward without him.

I didn't know how to move forward now.

What was there out there for me? Getting fired from *Good Morning, New Jersey* had taught me that it was harder to find a new job than I thought. And that's when my record had been spotless. Now? Now I'd killed an entire show.

Who would have me now?

I curled into an even tighter ball and looked at my alarm clock. It was seven o'clock. I had six and a half hours to figure out what to say to them. I had six and a half hours to figure out what to do.

Six.

Five.

Four.

Three.

Two.

One.

When I got to work, I still hadn't figured it out. Plus, I had the handy-dandy addition of giant raccoon eyes, frayed nerves, and a profound inability to be logical.

After our morning meeting, I told Lenny I was in the middle of something, and let him take over in the control room while I attempted to map out a strategy. But the lack of sleep wasn't helping me do what I hadn't been able to the previous evening. How do you strategize utter failure?

I paced in my office. I paced in the restroom. I paced in the control room when no one was looking. In fact, I was in the middle of a particularly frantic bout of pacing when I caught sight of Merv in deep conference with the stage manager, Pete.

"What's going on now?" I asked.

"Mike's offended by a word in the next story," he explained.

"Offended?" I narrowed my eyes. "It's about Easter chicks."

"It's okay," Merv said. "They're on commercial break, and we've sent someone for a thesaurus."

A thesaurus? Oh, *hell* no.

Apparently, I wasn't the only one who felt that way, to judge from Colleen's shrill response when Pete approached the news desk, *Roget's* in hand.

"He needs synonyms now?" She threw up her hands in disgust.

"Okay," said the stage manager. "We've got 'feathery,' 'fleecy,' 'flocculent'...."

"'Flocculent' sounds like something we'd hear out of Lisa's mouth," Lenny grumbled.

But Mike didn't hear any others he liked, either. "I'm not going to say 'fluffy,'" he insisted. "It's bad enough that I have to do these ridiculous stories. There are certain words I will not utter on air."

"Hey, buddy," drawled Colleen. "Last week I had to use 'rectal' and 'moisture' in the same sentence."

"Well, first dates are always awkward."

She glared at him. "I didn't see anyone coming at *me* with reference material," Colleen went on, undaunted.

"Interesting point," said Mike. "Blow me."

She rolled her eyes. "Yeah, that's happening."

"Blooooooooow meeeeee." His microphone made the words echo across the studio.

"Kill his mike!" Merv shouted. We didn't want a repeat of Jimmy Carter.

All right. Enough was enough. I pressed the button that connected us to their earpieces. "Mike."

He ignored me.

I tried again, louder. "Mike!"

He popped out his earpiece and pointedly scratched his temple with his middle finger.

That was *it*. I sprang out of my chair.

"Becky?" Lenny said in warning. "What are you doing?"

Fueled by fury, I stomped into the studio and up to the news desk. "I need to talk to you," I spat at Mike.

"Um, Becky?" As if from a great distance, I heard Pete. "We're back in sixty seconds...."

"I've looked up to you all my life," I said to Mike. "Idolized you. My dad and I used to watch you on TV." If he dared make some snotty comment about how I'd told him that in the elevator, I'd . . . "You epitomized the best of what I wanted to do." What I'd failed to do. "So imagine my surprise—" You know what? Adam was wrong. "—When it turned out that you're the *worst person in the world*." Not number three, not number two. The absolute worst.

He looked at me, stunned momentarily into silence.

"Do you have any *idea* how lucky you are to be here?" My voice went up an octave. "How lucky we *all are* to have these jobs? How quickly it could all be *taken away*?"

I doubted he cared. After all, his contract would remain intact long after *Daybreak* was hoisted into its coffin.

Dimly, I realized everyone in the studio was staring, but I was long past paltry concerns like dignity.

"Um, we're back in thirty," said Pete.

Everyone on set had stopped in their tracks.

"Uh, Becky?" I heard Lenny's voice shine out from the control room. "You okay?"

"This was going to be my dream job," I ranted to Mike. "My dream *life*! Working on a network show in New York City."

"Uh-oh," said Merv. "I think Pomeroy broke her."

"Becky," Lenny said again. "In fifteen—"

"And there's a guy—a great guy, who is actually kind of *smokin'*—and he can stand me long enough to have *sex with me*."

Mike's eyes widened just the tiniest bit at that one. All around the studio, I could hear the gasps. Colleen's smile was real for once. She was loving the show.

"Becky," Lenny pleaded. "In five—"

"And instead," I said, or rather, screamed, "it's all a mess.

Because of you." I jabbed a finger at him. "No one here does their job well because *you can't be bothered to do yours at all!*"

I glared at Mike. His face was frozen. No one in the room dared to breathe—but me. I sucked in oxygen like it was going out of style.

"And, we're back," said Pete the stage manager.

slinked off the set, still hyperventilating, as Colleen snapped into host mode.

"Welcome back to *Daybreak*," she said cheerily. "And now, with a check of the weather, here's Ernie on the plaza."

The feed switched to a shot of our ebullient weatherman standing in front of a thick crowd of people. "Thanks, Colleen. Well, we're all enjoying the sunshine out here today."

The folks behind Ernie jostled one another and toasted plastic cups filled with lemonade. "*Daybreak!*" one screamed. "Woo-hoo!"

I knew for a fact that there were only six people in that crowd. Six people artfully arranged inside the camera's frame to look like a pack of hundreds. Each of the six had been given free lemonade, hot dogs, and IBS T-shirts in exchange for their efforts.

Ernie smiled at the camera. "Makes me wish I was wearing

my thong." He laughed merrily. The fabricated crowd laughed too.

I felt hollow. Hollow and helpless. I trailed down the hallways, ignoring the stunned expressions of the people I passed along the way. The executive producer of *Daybreak* had just had a nervous breakdown in front of her entire staff. Had my rant gone on another microsecond, I would have been doing it in front of our audience as well.

All four of them.

I climbed into the elevator and pressed the button for the lobby. I needed to feel some of that sun Ernie promised on my face.

At one of the sub floors, the elevator stopped, and an intern climbed on. He took one look at me, and hugged the edge of the elevator. Ditto for the archivist we met on the next floor.

I gave them a little wave. "Uh, hi?"

They exchanged glances, and sidled even farther away.

I had a very bad feeling about this. Either I was wearing the crazy on my face or . . . oh God. How many people had been watching the in-house feed monitors when I went on my little tirade?

The door opened at the lobby and my two companions watched me the way one might a rabid dog. "Are you . . . getting off?" one asked me.

"Um . . ." My voice came out high and brittle. "Not yet." I jammed my finger against the button leading to Adam's floor. The other two raced out of the elevator.

I got the same response as I walked through the news department. Some people stared. A few of them scattered. I kept my chin up and my eyes straight ahead. *Just get to Adam's of-*

fice, and don't think about how whatever reputation I had at IBS ten minutes ago—hard-ass? failure? fangirl?—had now mutated into something far more humiliating.

I opened the door to *7 Days*. The people there were clustered in groups that got quiet as soon as they caught sight of me. Oh, no. Oh no no no no no.

With great trepidation, I approached Adam's door and knocked. He answered, a triumphant smile practically splitting his face in two. "Hey, cutie," he said. "You're nuts, you know that?"

I nodded miserably.

"Let's go to lunch."

I stared at him. "It's not even ten A.M."

He shrugged. "Brunch, then. Come on. You need to get out of here for a bit." He grabbed my hand and drew me back down the hall. We were only getting stared at more.

"Adam . . . ," I said in warning.

He looked back and me and winked. "Nothing's a secret around here, Becky. It's a newsroom. And you're always on *Candid Camera*."

We made it out of the building in one piece, though my cheeks felt heated by the time we exited the lobby onto the plaza.

"I thought it was a nice gesture, for what it's worth," Adam said. "Some people send flowers, you yell at giant cameras."

I was too shell-shocked to respond.

"That *was* me you were talking about, right?"

I pulled my hand from his so I could rub my temples. "I'm never going to be able to show my face in there again."

"Nonsense," said Adam, steering me down a side street

161

toward a diner. "Everyone was on your side. Mike doesn't deserve you. You know that. We all know it. He's ungrateful and nasty."

"Can't argue with you on that anymore."

He smiled. "Glad to see you upgraded him from my personal threat level."

I forced a chuckle.

"It's making you crazy," he said. We stopped walking for a moment and he turned to face me. "*He's* making you crazy. It's not worth it."

I gaped at him in disbelief. Not worth it? The news? My dream job? Well, what was left of it anyway.

"Becky, I know you think it's a great job, but it is just a job. There are other shows you could work for. . . ."

Easy for him to say, with his connections and his education and his track record of never killing a television show almost half a century old. Adam Bennett, of the *Newsweek* Bennetts, would find another show to work for. But Becky Fuller of the Weehawken Fullers? Not so much.

"I get it," I said stiffly. "You think my life is ridiculous. My show is ridiculous. I'm ridiculous. . . ."

"I never said that—"

"You're upstairs doing investigative pieces on Zimbabwe and Zaire and—" Crap, what else started with a Z?

"Zambia?" Adam suggested.

"*Zambia!*" I cried. "God, you hard news guys look down on us! You, and Mike—"

"Whoa," Adam said, holding up his hands in protest. "Do *not* lump me in the same category as—"

"What is it, huh?" I asked. "Is it because our audience is women?"

"Hold on," said Adam. "I'm not the one who looks down

on you, remember? Your show serves the needs of its audience. So does mine. So does the nightly news. If all news shows were the same, why would we need so many?"

I bit my lip. Did he have to sound so damn *reasonable* while I was in the middle of my rant?

"Yeah, Mike thinks it's all bullshit. Mike—who, I might add, you literally hunted down to force him on your show. Did you think he was dying to go back on air and do pieces about how your hamster might be giving you salmonella?"

Wow, Adam. From a compliment to a punch in three short sentences. Impressive. Good thing he'd softened me up for that blow, otherwise I might not even have felt it, given the day I'd had.

"Salmonella," I said slowly, "is a very serious health concern. There are over forty thousand cases of it diagnosed each year. I'm sorry if you or Mike think it's a waste of your time."

Adam sighed. "Becky, come on. You just need to have a little perspective here. Give it some time. . . ."

Time? That was rich. "I don't *have* time," I said, blinking my eyes to wick away my traitorous tears. "This is the only chance I'm ever going to have to do this job." And I'd already lost it. *I'd already lost it.* But I was still the only one who knew that.

"That's not true," Adam insisted.

And how could I tell Adam? I could trust him not to gossip about me to IBS—it wasn't that. But I couldn't bear to admit to him that I'd failed. How would I ever convince myself I was good enough for him then?

I shook my head. "You don't get it. How can you? They hired me to be incompetent."

"You're *not* incompetent."

Oh, yes I was. If only Adam knew. No—if only there were

a way to keep him from *ever* knowing. "I've got to make this work," I said, more to myself than to him. "I've got to. I'll do it over my dead body if I have to."

Adam's expression took on some of the wary characteristics I'd seen on the faces of the people back at the office. Had I really gone around the bend? Was the crazy showing on my face now?

Of course. I was standing on a public street railing—at *Adam*, of all people. Adam, who'd never been anything but kind to me. Adam, who was exactly who he said he was, who did respect the work I was doing. Who, moreover, respected *me*, whether or not I was the executive producer at *Daybreak*. Or anywhere.

I sighed, walked over to him, and placed a kiss on his nose. "I'm sorry," I said. "I didn't mean to blow up at you, too."

He looked at me, sympathetic, but not pitying. "Bloody Marys with brunch?"

I nodded. "Definitely."

There was something magic in the Bloody Mary. Either that, or spending time with Adam was far more restorative than I'd thought, even when we kept all our clothes on. Because by the end of brunch, I had started feeling a little bit like my old self again. The girl who could fire Paul McVee. The girl who could drag Mike Pomeroy onto *Daybreak* like a big game hunter with a trophy.

Maybe I would go down, but I'd go down swinging.

When we returned to the IBS building, I went straight to Jerry's office. His assistant, possibly wondering if I'd gone postal, tried to head me off at the pass.

"Um, you don't have an appointment—" She jumped in front of me.

I stood my ground. "I'm from Jersey and I have a pepper spray key chain. Now *step aside*."

"Coke or Diet Coke?" she asked meekly.

I blew past her and burst into Jerry's office. Jerry was sitting at his desk, doing paperwork. He didn't even look up as I entered.

"What now?" he asked, bored. "Going to bust a cap in my ass?"

"What if I get the ratings up?" I said, a little too breathless for my taste, but it got the point across.

Now Jerry lifted his head. And he didn't look happy.

"We have six weeks," I went on. "What if we move the needle enough?"

"You won't," he said, and returned to his work.

"You don't know that."

Jerry sighed and laid down his pen. "Becky . . ."

I drew closer to the desk. "There must be some number we can hit that would give us a shot. An extra six months, something."

"Well sure," said Jerry, in a tone that suggested there must also be some chance that the office furniture would suddenly get up and dance the tango. "If you got something absurd. Over a 1.5—"

"Done." I smacked the desktop and turned on my heel. "I have your word," I said as I headed for the door. "If the ratings go up more than three quarters of a point, we get more time."

"Won't happen!" Jerry called after me.

I paused at the door. "We'll see about that," I said. And as long as I was going to be making demands . . . "Oh, and by the way. Your girlfriend, Lisa? Get her a dictionary and stick her on someone else's show. She's killing me."

If we were out, his little bit on the side was going to need a new job anyway. So might as well get her used to the idea now.

And then I breezed out. I had a lot of work to do.

By the next morning, I had everything in place. It helped that the *Daybreak* staff was terrified of me again. But I didn't care. If I had to work from a place of fear to get these people in line, then so be it.

I was going to give them a potent illustration of my new management style this morning.

"There you are," Lenny said when I arrived at the studio, slightly windswept but ready for action. "Where have you been?"

I crossed the room and grabbed the schedule off the desk. "We're changing some things."

"We are?" he asked. "Should I be worried?"

I turned to Merv. "Is Ernie in place?"

Merv checked the feed from the remote. "Um, I'm not really sure what I'm looking at. . . ."

Now Lenny did look concerned. "Ernie's supposed to be interviewing people as they come off the roller coaster—"

"No," I said firmly. "Not anymore he's not."

Ernie, bless his simple, good-natured heart, had been pretty sanguine about my idea. Then again, I hadn't given him much of an opportunity to say no.

"Merv," I said, "the camera's remote-operated. Why don't you widen out a little."

Merv and Lenny exchanged glances, then the director did as he was told.

"Jesus Christ," Lenny said, and crossed himself. His faith, I was learning, was a mysterious and fluid thing.

Ernie was no longer standing in front of the roller coaster. He was strapped inside.

"It's called picking up the game, people," I said, as everyone in the studio turned to look at me. "From now on, every story we do will be undeniable. We may not be the *Today* show, or *Good Morning America*, or whatever that show on CBS is called—"

Oh, God. Was I losing it again? No matter. It was too late, and maybe what we needed was a little lunacy. What was the line I was looking for? Oh, yeah: *I'm mad as hell, and I'm not going to take it anymore.*

"We will work *harder*, we will be more *aggressive*, and we will do it *now*."

Lenny looked on in horror. "Are you going to—"

"No," I said. "I'm not going to sing. Now"—I pointed at the screen—"make sure the audio's working."

Merv obeyed. Lenny shook his head. "So what? So he has a heart attack we'll be able to capture every heart-rending scream?"

Exactly. I pressed the button to turn on the speaker to Ernie's intercom. "Ernie? Feeling okay?"

He smiled at the camera and gave me a thumbs-up.

"See?" I said. "He's happy."

"Dumb people are often happy," Lenny replied, frowning deeply.

"Lucky them," I said. "Now let's go."

On set, Colleen began introducing Ernie's segment. "Thrill seekers have something to look forward to this summer as Six Flags unveils a brand-new roller coaster. The Manhandler is the fastest coaster in the United States, with speeds of up to a hundred and thirty miles an hour and a ninety-five-degree angle of descent."

Lenny gave me a dubious glance. Just offscreen, Mike sat at his news desk, arms folded, his expression far more than dubious. Closer to "disgusted."

Colleen was still talking. "Today, our own Ernie Appleby is getting a sneak peek at this amazing new ride. Isn't that right, Ernie?"

The monitors all switched to Ernie on the coaster. His legs dangled out of the bottom of the harness, his pants awkwardly hiked up, revealing pasty, surprisingly hairless calves.

Also, mismatched socks. I turned my eyes heavenward, then realized, remembering Ernie's fan base, that they'd probably find that endearing as well.

"Yes, it's exciting," Ernie was saying. "We've strapped the camera to our seat so that now, courtesy of *Daybreak*, you're about to see, along with me, exactly what this ride is like!" In the background, you could hear the steady *chug-chug-chug* as the car was pulled up the first hill. "So far," he said, looking around, "it's quite a beautiful ride. I've got an amazing view from up here. All blue sky except for a few cumulus clouds . . ."

In the control room, a few people snickered. Leave it to Ernie to work a weather report into a story about a roller coaster. What was next, a statement about the windchill factor?

"I'm heading for the first loop now!" he called.

"Good luck, Ernie," Colleen said.

The coaster car continued chugging, the sound growing faster and higher as Ernie reached the crest. Puffy white cumulus clouds framed his face. He looked like a Renaissance cherub. Well, if Raphael had ever painted one strapped to a vinyl roller coaster seat.

"This is so exhilarating!" Ernie was saying. "This is—"

The chugging stopped. The camera pulled tight on Ernie's face. Screams started up in the background as Ernie's smile vanished, replaced by a look of stark terror.

"Oh my God," he cried. "Ohmygodohmygod."

"Yeah, no," Lenny said to me. "It's a great idea."

According to the diagram I'd seen of the Manhandler, Ernie should be falling into his first of three barrel rolls by now.

"FUUUUUUUUUUUUUUUUUUUUUUUUU—," Ernie screamed.

Merv dived toward the mute button. "Got it."

But Ernie was apparently still screaming his head off on-screen. We watched him twist around the loops, his hair flying up and down, his jowls flapping in the g-force as he spun. It was incredible. It was stunning.

I hoped people were seeing this. Otherwise, it was entirely possible I'd just killed my meteorologist on a whim.

"Has he stopped cussing?" I asked Merv. He turned on internal audio. "Mommy!" Ernie was crying. "Mommy! Help me!"

I laughed. "Okay, you gotta put that one on."

"You got it." Merv flipped the switch.

A few moments later, the ride was done. We watched Ernie, chest heaving, eyes wide and watery, pull around the final corner of the coaster and back to the loading zone. His hair was blown off his face, his cheeks and nose were pink.

"Ernie?" Colleen asked nervously. "How you doing?"

A huge smile broke out on the meteorologist's face. "Can I go again?"

16

Everyone was riding high that afternoon. Everyone, that
was, except Mike.

He stormed off after the broadcast, sat in stony silence
during our lunch meeting, then cornered me afterward at the
Craft Services corridor.

"How is this journalism?" he cried. I was surprised he wasn't
shaking his fist at me. "What are you going to do to him next?
Plant electrodes on his balls?"

"To what end?" I asked calmly, as if I were genuinely
curious.

This only infuriated him more. Good. "You know, I actually feel sorry for that animatronic puppet asshole."

"Don't waste your pity," I shot back. "Ernie's thrilled.
We've got eighty thousand hits on YouTube already. *And*"—a
fact that was much more important to me—"a bump in the
minute-to-minutes. He's a superstar."

"He's a clown," Mike corrected.

"Lighten up." I surveyed the muffin selection. Pretty picked over, by this point. The only ones left were bran. And no Danishes. Darn.

"You know what I've noticed?" Mike leaned in, voice lowered. "People only say 'lighten up' when they've got their fist up your ass."

Really? IBS execs basically had their fists up mine, but I hadn't heard anything of the sort. I turned to face him. "I hate to break this to you, Mike, but the fact is, the nation—no, the *world*—has debated news versus entertainment for years." I slapped a muffin on my plate. "Guess what? Your side *lost*."

"You're wrong." For once, Mike looked as angry as I felt. "People are smart. They want information, not junk—which is all you want to give them." He picked up a glazed donut and waved it in my face. "Junk! Sugar, sugar, and more sugar."

I picked up my muffin. "What do *you* want them to do?" I shoved my muffin at him. "Eat bran all day? Fiber, fiber, fiber?"

We shook our foodstuffs in each other's faces for a moment more, until we were interrupted by Lenny. He cleared his throat and reached past us for an apple. "This is an awesome work environment," he said.

I put down my muffin and took a deep breath, hoping to bring my status down from *lunatic* to merely *stressed*. "We have to get ratings, Mike. We have to, or we can have a lot of high-minded ideals and *not be on the air*." Didn't he remember what that was like? Not being on the air? Not doing any news at all, no matter how silly or petty some of it might seem? Wasn't this better than nothing?

Why couldn't I make him see that?

I stepped even closer to him. "This show might go down, Mike, but not because I'm not trying my hardest. Do you hear me? I don't care what you do anymore, but *I am not giving up.*"

"And then, when he started screaming?" Anna giggled and took another sip of her chardonnay. I'd invited her over to my postage-stamp apartment for a girls' night in. "Man, that was brilliant. I don't know how you got around him cussing like that."

"Apparently the amount of time between the F and the muted K was so long, the IBS lawyers classified it as separate and distinct utterances." I reached for the bottle balanced precariously on the edge of my storage chest–cum–coffee table and poured its last few drops into my glass.

"We must have watched it five times at work. Classic Becky Fuller."

Classic? I raised my eyebrows. I'd never strapped Harold the Hip-Hop Meteorologist into a roller coaster at *Good Morning, New Jersey*. Though maybe if I had, he would have stopped rapping. Perhaps I should suggest it to Anna.

"How is work?" I asked her instead.

"Fine." Anna shrugged. "Chip's sort of in-the-box about things. And we did have to explain to him where New Providence was last week. He thought we were talking about Rhode Island."

I groaned. "Didn't he think to bring a map with him when he took the job?"

"Guy's not from Jersey," said Anna. "He'll catch up. Sometime."

"Sometime before you leave?" I asked.

She laughed. "Why, Becky? You hiring?"

"I wish I were!" It would be great to have Anna back on

172

my team. Just talking to her over a bottle of wine was doing wonders for my mood. But even if I did manage to buy the show an extra few months to improve ratings, there's no way I'd have the ability to buy it a new producer.

Anna rose from the couch and walked two steps to the far wall. "Becks, I'm going to level with you. Your apartment would fit in my driveway."

"My apartment would fit in the car I had to sell to afford it," I replied. "This is not news. What kind of news show employee are you?" I shook the wine bottle, upside down, over my glass.

"Clearly not one doing my investigative best," she replied. "I haven't grilled you about this Adam guy yet."

"Adam," I said, "is dreamy."

She hopped back on the couch. "Go on!"

"And sweet. And smart. And supportive."

"Adam," she said, "is imaginary."

I laughed. "Actually, you know when I realized I really liked him?"

She leaned in, eyes alight. There was nothing Anna Garcia liked more than a good romance. It's why she had so many of them. "When?"

"When he answered his BlackBerry in the middle of our first date."

She blinked in disbelief. "He *what?*"

"I know!" I grinned. "I realized then we were perfect for each other."

"So he's as crazy as you, is what you're saying." Anna polished off her glass.

I stared into the bottom of mine, thinking of what I had planned for tomorrow. "No, honey. No one's quite as crazy as me."

. . .

Early the next morning, I was staked out in front of a ritzy apartment building on Central Park West. My sources told me that this target—a hot hip-hop artist sure to drive up ratings—tended to sleep in late. I drank an entire large coffee while waiting, but then started to worry that this wasn't such a great idea. Maybe he'd prefer if I went for vitamin water?

I watched folks go in and out of the building, and each time, my hopes rose, but it was never him. Finally, when I'd almost given up and gone in search of a bathroom—large coffee, remember?—I saw my prey exit his building and head for a waiting black Cadillac Escalade.

I raced to intercept him. "Excuse me!" I called, then froze. Should I call him by his real name? His stage name? What was appropriate here?

The man in question turned and gave me a deadpan glare. For some reason, the only thing I could think of was how this dude had been in prison. What was it with me and stalking folks who carried firearms?

"Sorry to bother you," I said quickly to my target. "I'm a big, big fan."

"You."

"Oh yeah." I snapped my fingers and started to sing. I have to admit, I'm not much of a rapper.

"Yeah, I've heard that one," he said, his tone flat.

"Such a classic," I said. "Anyway—my name is Becky Fuller, and I'm the executive producer at *Daybreak?*"

"At what?"

"Wow, you're funny, too!" I exclaimed with false cheer. "We'd love to have you on our show. We'll give you twice as

174

much time as *Today* and we'll let you sing four songs from your new album. Think about it."

He squinted. "What's your show?"

"*Daybreak?* On IBS?"

"Oh, uh . . . yeah." By which he meant, "Oh, uh . . . no."

I handed him my card. "Give me a call anytime. We'd love to have you!"

"Right." He stuck the card in his pants pocket and climbed into his chauffeur-driven car.

I held back my squeal and dance of triumph until after he pulled away.

The next day at *Daybreak*, we readied ourselves for Ernie's next "Atmospheric Adventure." The segment title had actually been Sasha's idea, but I liked it. Tied his official duties in with our new angle.

At least we had the pattern down pat. Once again the shot was tight on Ernie's face and upper torso. The viewer could tell he was being strapped into something. The viewer could tell he was nervous. But what the viewer couldn't tell was what was about to happen.

"Stay tuned," said Colleen, "for Ernie's latest 'Atmospheric Adventure.' "

If our new YouTube followers and Facebook friends were anything to judge by, they would. The minute-to-minutes looked good, and I was keeping my fingers crossed that the next ratings report would bear out the trend.

When we returned to Ernie, the shot zoomed out as we heard him say, "These fighter jets exert amazing stress on their passengers, with g-force measurements sometimes reaching—"

A loud whine filled the screen as the engines roared and Ernie took off. His smile wavered at the edges as the plane tilted back.

"All right, guys, here we go! Here we go, folks! Here we—"

"Um, boss?" Merv asked. "Do we cut away for barf?"

"Yes," I said. "But that's going to be a vomit-only policy. Hold on a nosebleed."

"Got it."

On-screen, Ernie was starting to freak out. "Oh fuuuuuu . . ."

"Cut the sound," I cued. Merv cut.

But then, better than a nosebleed, and prettier than vomit, we got our money shot: Ernie fainted dead away.

I was going over the minute-to-minutes when Colleen caught up with me in the hallway. She didn't look pleased.

"I need to talk to you," she said. "About Ernie."

I eyed her with suspicion. Had Mike somehow gotten to her? Was she about to give me some ridiculous impassioned speech about the sanctity of the news?

"You too?" I sighed. "Why is everyone so worried about him? He's a grown man, he's signed all the release forms, his life insurance is totally paid up—"

"You bet I'm worried," Colleen said. "Ernie's a hack and you know it. Yet you keep giving him all the good stuff."

I stopped walking and gave her my full attention.

"I would have *killed* on that coaster," said Colleen. "And tomorrow's bungee expedition? Come on now. Who'd you rather see scream?"

She had a point there. She might even have those magic

176

three quarters of a point we'd need to keep the show on the air.

Colleen came closer. "Look, I see what you're doing and I think it's great. It's exactly what I've been waiting for. Put me in, Coach. Sign me up. Whatever you want to call it. I'm in."

I smiled. "Great," I said. "Any particular ideas?"

Colleen rubbed her hands together with glee. "Well, now that you mention it . . ."

The following day brought a special treat to early morning pedestrians passing by the IBS plaza. Colleen Peck, coanchor of the morning show *Daybreak*, was decked out in an enormous foam rubber sumo wrestler's suit, grappling in a makeshift ring with an actual sumo wrestler.

Lenny and I watched the proceedings from the control room. His expression remained doubtful.

"What?" I said, gesturing to the screen. Behind Colleen's fake girth, I could see a steady crowd forming. Some of them were on their cell phones, no doubt informing their friends and family back home that they just had to turn on IBS. Others were holding up said cell phones, trying to get their own video record of the event. It was a certifiable success.

"She's . . . *grunting* an awful lot, don't you think?" Lenny asked, wrinkling his upper lip.

Grunting? Great. I turned to Merv. "Can you hike up the sound?"

The day after that, we had happy fun animal time in the studio. Sasha was in seventh heaven as she ushered the animal handler onto the living room set, where Colleen was primed and waiting. We'd had to pack on a little extra makeup to hide the bruises this morning, but she was a sport about it. Who knew sumo wrestlers were that tough?

Colleen introduced our guest and her charge: a tiny little squirrel-looking thing called a sugar glider. Apparently, they were all the rage as celebrity pets.

"These are adorable," Colleen cooed as the handler held the creature out to the camera. "So, they're marsupials?"

I pressed the button that turned on Colleen's headset. "Pick it up," I suggested.

Colleen obeyed.

The handler looked mildly alarmed. "You just want to be careful you don't bring them too close to your face."

Colleen cast a quick glance at me, then nestled the marsupial against her cheek. "Aww, it's so soft. You cute widdle—"

The sugar glider wriggled out of Colleen's grasp, then vanished up the arm of her blazer. She shrieked and began hopping around the set, desperately attempting to shake the animal loose from the strap of her bra.

Eventually, she fished it out of her cleavage. "Well," she said, holding the creature at arm's length, "aren't they a fun time for the whole family."

Score.

The Web buzz was building to match the minute-to-minutes and the latest ratings report was showing a very definite—if very slight—bump. This was working. I just had to keep it up. Push the envelope a little further.

The day after that, Colleen participated in a tumbling act with a bunch of local children who were part of a dance troupe that raised money for charities. Usual fare for the morning show crowd, to be sure, but Colleen kicked it up a notch by dressing like the children in a Pepto-Bismol pink body stocking and matching giant tutu.

Her YouTube hits began to give Ernie's a run for his money.

I avoided Mike as much as possible. There were only so many stony glares of disapproval a girl could take. He kept delivering the news in his usual dry manner, and his expressions of disgust at my tactics, both on and off set, were so ubiquitous as to have grown invisible. No one even paid attention to him anymore. And why would they, when they could watch the infinitely more entertaining spectacle of Ernie Appleby getting a tattoo on his ass.

Yes. Tattoo. Ass. Live television. God, I'm good.

Ernie was such a sport. He sat there on the table, all relevant parts covered except for one creamy, broadcast-friendly flank.

My meteorologist addressed the camera with equanimity, holding up a sketch of a tornado with two lightning bolts coming out the top. "The thing is, tattoos can be quite painful, depending on the sensitivity of the area you're stabbing with a needle." He chuckled. "Which is why I'm choosing a place with a little extra padding."

The tattoo artist stuck him with the needle.

Ernie's expression turned resigned and then: "Oh, fuuuuuuu—"

Merv cut the sound.

As soon as the segment was over, we returned to the studio, where Mike looked like he'd spent the break chomping on rotted meat. "When we come back, we'll tell you all about new ways to cope with"—he grimaced, forcing himself to spit out the words—"menopause."

Served him right.

I didn't even care. According to the ratings sheet, we'd already gone up a quarter point. Just another half to go.

Next up, we had booked that hip-hop artist, thanks to my unheard-of generosity when it came to amount of performance time, and on the living room set Colleen bopped along while he performed one of his latest hits. The rapper kept casting her confused glances, sidling away from this crazy middle-aged white woman who also chimed in whenever he hit the chorus.

After the show, Lenny saw me giving instructions to a crew of carpenters. "What's going on now?" he asked.

I grinned at him. "New doorknobs."

"You're kidding!" Lenny whistled. "How'd you find room for it in the budget?"

"I didn't. Oh, by the way, make room in the schedule tomorrow for Colleen's new segment on 'Home Repair You Need to Call the Experts For.'"

One of the carpenters looked over and gave me a callused thumbs-up.

"We're going to have a few local carpenters on to explain why."

"Of course we are," Lenny said. "Of course. So, on the CEO story, did you want the transvestite prostitute to come on dressed as a man or a woman?"

I considered it. "Man. No. Woman."

"Because it might be more of a shock—"

"I know!" I cried. "Have him/her do the first segment as a woman, then boom! After the break, he/she comes back as a man. What do you think?"

"I like it." Lenny made a mark on his sheet. "I mean, for your dastardly purposes, not for the betterment of humanity."

"Shut up, Mike Pomeroy," I replied.

"You got it, boss." He turned to go, then stopped. "Oh, we got the footage from the Irish Famine Memorial."

I bounced. "How is it?"

"Colleen is the worst bagpiper in the history of the world."

Perfect. "And the outfit?"

"Even more ridiculous." Lenny sighed. "Are you sure you know what you're doing here, Becky? Are we making fools out of ourselves?"

"No," I said. "We were already fools. Now I'm just trying to turn that impression to our benefit."

I could only hope it would work.

17

"Our demos are getting better," I said as Adam handed me a box of lo mein, "but our overall numbers are not where they need to be." We were having a quiet evening in at Adam's apartment, sitting on the couch, eating takeout while the TV droned on in the background. I wouldn't have traded this for the VIP Room of any club in Manhattan. After all, they didn't have Adam.

"Hmmm . . . ," he said, and dipped his egg roll in the plum sauce. "Might be time for another eight-part series on the orgasm."

"You think so?" I asked, chopsticks partway to my mouth. "What new angle could—" I stopped. Adam was grinning at me. "Oh, I see." I nudged his foot with my stockinged one. "You're making fun of me."

He gave me a lopsided smirk. "If you want, though, I'd be happy to help you come up with new angles."

"Maybe later." I dug into my food. "Can't miss *Nightly News*."

"Sadly," Adam said, looking down at his dish, "with you that's not a joke. You really would prefer news to sex."

"That's not true."

"Oh yeah?" He started counting off on his fingers. "The first night you spent here I found you sneaking a visit to MSNBC.com in the middle of the night. Last week, you canceled our date to stake out a source, which"—he held up his hand—"I was totally sympathetic to. Then the other night, I spent twenty minutes trying to get you to pay more attention to me than to Rachel Maddow."

"She was doing a really interesting piece on—"

"Rachel Maddow," Adam said, "already has a girlfriend. I'd like to keep mine to myself."

I caught my breath. *"Girlfriend?"*

He looked up at me. "Yeah. She's—"

"No," I said. "I mean, you called me your girlfriend. I . . . I didn't know we were doing that."

"Oh." There was something endearingly sheepish in his voice. "Well, *I* am. Hope you don't mind."

"No," I said. "It's great." And then, "You're kind of obsessed with the soft serve, huh? I mean, first you ask me out on a date without asking me out on a date, and then I'm your girlfriend before I know about it."

He grinned. "Eat your noodles."

I grinned back and did as I was told. After a minute, I picked up the remote. "Can I just put on CNN for, like, a minute? There might be something on that serial killer who Twittered his victims—"

He grunted and didn't look my way.

"You're right," I said quickly. I turned the TV off and

placed the remote control firmly back on the coffee table. "It's not important. I'll worry about it tomorrow."

I was rewarded for my restraint with the reassuring touch of his hand on my thigh, and I snuggled up against him. The news could wait. It could totally wait. Was I such an addict that I couldn't turn it off for an hour or two and spend some time with a smart, funny, totally smokin' guy who liked me enough to not only want to have dinner with me and sex with me—*more than once*—but also to call me his girlfriend? Was this addiction what came of doing nothing but watching the news at night—every night? Did I not know how to survive without it?

When we were done with dinner, we went together to the kitchen to clean up the dishes and glasses. I was scraping some stray bits of fried rice down the sink when I felt Adam's arms curl around me from behind. Something warm welled up inside and I leaned against his chest, reveling in the way he felt pressed up against my back. This wasn't so bad. I could even get used to it. Stop worrying about proving myself, leave the work at the office for once. Evenings like this made me wonder what my life would be like if I could make this happen. What if I brought up the ratings the full three quarters of a point? What if I turned *Daybreak* into . . . well, not a hit show, but a solid performer? Something steady and strong that could stay on-air for another forty-seven years. I'd have proven I could do it. I'd be a successful executive producer. That would be enough, right? I'd move into a nicer apartment in Manhattan—maybe with Adam. Heck, if he kept up his current MO and I retained my general cluelessness about relationships, I probably wouldn't realize we were cohabitating until a few weeks after we'd signed a lease and moved in.

Oh my God, I couldn't believe I was fantasizing about moving in with Adam. It was way too early for any of those daydreams. Way too early to spend time imagining what an unbearably cute television news power couple we would become.

There I went again. And it wasn't helping any that Adam was placing warm, openmouthed kisses on my neck now. It wasn't helping that I inhaled his scent with every breath. I turned in his arms and pressed my lips against his. I wrapped my hands around his neck and tilted my head so we could get even closer. He backed me up against the sink, his legs sliding between mine. My eyes fluttered open, which was when I saw it, right outside Adam's kitchen window.

The neighbor's TV. Showing CNN.

Adam's breath had quickened, and I moved my attentions from his mouth to his throat. I planted some feather-light kisses on his collarbone, but I kept my eyes trained on the TV. Were they doing the segment on the serial killer yet?

Adam's fingers skimmed beneath my shirt, and he moaned a little. My angle wasn't quite right to see the screen. I wiggled a few inches to the side, one eye on my boyfriend, one looking through the window. There, that was better.

"So," he whispered. "Bedroom, or right here on the counter?"

"Mmmm . . . ," I said vaguely. Okay, this was better, but still not perfect. What was the chyron saying at the bottom of the screen?

Suddenly, I noticed that Adam had stopped kissing me.

"What are you doing?" he asked. He tried to swivel, but I was too quick and started tugging him out of the room.

"Come on," I coaxed. "Let's—"

He pulled his hand from mine and walked to the window. "Wow," he said, his voice flat. "You can see the neighbor's TV from here. And it's closed-captioned. Score!"

"Adam," I begged.

But he just shook his head. "That's really depraved."

I opened my mouth to protest, but then stopped. "You know what?" I said, nodding. "You're right."

He looked at me, baffled.

"You win. You caught me. I try to get every story. That's what I do." I blew out of the kitchen and grabbed my coat.

He followed me, "What are you doing?"

"You look at me like there's something wrong with me. All the time." Damn it, where were my shoes? The left one was under the couch, the right . . . I searched around the coffee table. "I can't do this. . . ."

Adam crossed his arms. "That's the most ridiculous statement you've ever made, and it's a tight race for that title."

I located my right shoe, shoved my foot into it, and flipped my head back up. Oh yeah? I was ridiculous as well as depraved, was I? "You don't understand," I cried. "It's so easy for you, but I can't let down my guard. Ever. We're still not booking the A-list unless we let them take over the whole show, and I'm not sure that's helping us with the casual fans, just the hard-core ones. And YouTube hits are great, but are they translating to ratings? I totally whiffed on getting an interview with the arsonist's mother—"

"Oh, Jesus," Adam said. He threw up his hands in frustration. "You're still obsessing over that?"

"Of course I am!" I crammed my arms into my jacket and shrugged it onto my shoulders. I can't miss *anything*. I make a mistake, I won't get another chance."

"Jesus." He ran his hands through his hair. "You have got to be a little bit easier on yourself."

"Why?" I asked. "No one else is. I have to work harder at this than—"

"Becky, this has nothing to do with reality," he said, frustrated. "This is just your ridiculous paranoia about your—"

"I'm not in the lucky white man's club with you and all the other morning show EPs and all the guys named Chip!"

"—Experience and education," Adam finished, as though I hadn't interrupted him.

I returned the favor. "I mean, who names their kid *Chip*? What *is* that?"

Adam didn't respond, just stared at me with an appalling mixture of shock and pity on his face. I was depraved. Ridiculous. Paranoid.

Perfect. Just Perfect. At least we were on the same page about what my failings were. "See?" I said, gesturing at him. "That's the look. That. I have to go." I grabbed my briefcase and practically raced to the door.

"Becky, wait a second."

His voice sounded so plaintive that, for a fraction of a second, I hesitated, my hand on the knob. But I couldn't. "I'm sorry," I said, and hurled myself out the door.

I was barely in the cab before I realized what a huge fucking mistake I'd just made. Again. I'd run out on Adam when I'd seen him with the blonde. And tonight, I ran out on him as soon as he prodded the giant, festering wound that was my career insecurity. *Chip!* I'd likened him to Chip and I'd picked a glimpse at a neighbor's television over the way he was kissing me and now I was sitting here in a dark cab that smelled vaguely of stale vomit instead of in Adam's bright and welcoming kitchen because I couldn't turn it off. Not for a single evening.

The in-taxi television announcer said, "An interesting development in California today—"

I switched the set off and looked out the window. See? I could do it.

I looked out on the dark Manhattan streets. It was early yet, so the sidewalks were still filled with people. Parents hurrying home to their children. Lovers on their way to a rendezvous. Newsmakers on their way to give me some content. I sighed and turned the TV back on. Who the hell was I kidding?

As it turned out, the development in California was not very interesting at all. Of course not. It was taxicab news. Only a step or two up from my own miserable excuse for a show. My own bit of mass-media-pandering newstainment. My—what had Mike called it?—horseshit. The horseshit that was my reason for living.

I trudged up the steps to my apartment and dropped my briefcase by the door. I trudged to bed, shedding my coat and shoes as I went. Out of reflex, I turned on the television on the counter, then the one on the bookshelf, then the one by my bedside table. I sat there, listening to the anchors drone on for a minute. There was nothing important. It was all just noise.

I shut them off, and for once, silence reigned in my apartment. I was utterly alone.

The next morning, I was surprised to discover that I wasn't the first person into work. Mike was already seated at his desk, his phone pressed to his ear, taking furious notes about something or other. I wondered if he was having some sort of issue with his stock portfolio. Or maybe he was planning some sort of supercool pheasant-hunting trip. Those were the only things I could imagine would get Mr. Clock Puncher Mike Pomeroy excited these days. It certainly wasn't the fact that I was forcing him to bake blueberry muffins with one of the runners-up from *Top Chef* next week.

It was a shame. If he could manage to get past his news snobbery, he had a lot to offer to a morning show audience. His life experiences were fascinating and his expertise was broad. He could bring so much to the broadcast, if only he got his head out of his ass. But that was a losing battle and one I was sick of trying to fight.

As I rounded the corner to my office, an intern caught up to me. "Ms. Fuller? These just came in." She held out a ratings sheet. I snatched them from her hands like an addict waiting for my fix. Maybe this was it. All the skydiving and the sumo wrestling and the horrible hoops I'd made my on-air talent jump through—maybe it had all paid off. I scanned the sheet.

Things had been looking so good. We were so close. More and more people were tuning in all the time. Our ratings had gone up . . . more than half a point.

But it wasn't enough. Not for the deal I'd made with my boss.

I slumped against the wall. There it was in black and white. Official. Irrefutable. I hadn't done it. A minute later the phone rang, and I knew even before I answered that it was Jerry, calling to discuss my abject failure.

Man, I hate it when I'm right.

"Have you seen the numbers?" he asked in his usual brisk style.

"Yes," I mumbled. I cleared my throat. Maybe I could try

to spin this. "They're much better. If you look at the trends, we've been really improving. We're way up from last year."

"So?"

"Come on," I begged. "I'm almost there. Only a quarter point to go. If we only had a little more time. I think if we maybe do that segment where Ernie—"

"Becky—" Jerry began.

I didn't want to beg, but what the hell? Humiliation was the order of the day at this morning show. "Please, Jerry. There are so many people who rely on this show. Who believe in it."

Jerry tsked through the phone. "You have until Friday. That was the deal we made. And those numbers—Becky: *They're just not good enough.*"

I floated through the next few hours like a ghost. I accepted the stories people pitched, signed off on requests for remote teams or guest gifts. It's possible I told Lenny he could buy a new espresso machine for Craft Services. What did it matter anyway? It wouldn't even be delivered by the time *Daybreak*'s days were done.

Done. Finished. *Finito*. And it was my fault.

I thought about the two-part series Sasha was putting together on endangered birds of prey. The piece Tracy had pitched about doing a mock *Project Runway* event at a local arts high school to drum up scholarship money for its flagging design program. I thought about Lenny and his two kids, and how Colleen had outlasted fourteen executive producers and half a dozen coanchors and was willing to make a fool of herself on-screen in order to keep her job. I thought about how Ernie had foolishly added the word "Daybreak" underneath his tornado tattoo. It was like getting the name of a lover inked on your body when said lover's already got one foot out the door.

Every single one of these people would soon be out of work. Some of them would land on their feet, sure. In fact, Ernie probably had a decent career ahead of him in the growing industry of late-night news show clowns. Jon Stewart had featured clips from "Atmospheric Adventures" so many times I half expected him to steal my meteorologist away. But as for the others . . . the prognosis wasn't too good.

On set, Colleen was wrapping up the latest segment. ". . . it turns out the burger patties were contaminated with E. coli, which can cause cramping and diarrhea. And we'll be right back on *Daybreak*."

The camera light went off, and Colleen wrinkled her pert nose. "Ooh, a story about uncontrollable shitting and look who gets it. Me."

"That's not my sort of thing," Mike said, tapping his notes into order against the desktop.

"Hey," Colleen snapped at him. "This is our *job*. You think you're above it? Maybe you *were*, before you were *fired*, but now you're down here in the muck with the rest of us."

A few of the producers looked over. I wondered if they were about to burst into applause.

"And yet I still have standards," Mike said, unfazed. "Unfortunately for you."

"Oh," Colleen said. "And I suppose I don't?"

"Sure you do. When you got your Pap smear on-air, you wore a robe. Classy touch."

She started in her seat. "You know, I've just about had it—"

"And we're back in five, four—," said the stage manager.

"You self-important, gaseous—"

192

"—Three, two, one—"

Mike didn't miss a beat. He turned to the camera. "Welcome back to *Daybreak*. Tomorrow on the show, Colleen will make the British classic 'bangers and mash' with chef Gordon Ramsay."

"That's right," she said coldly. Colleen! Cold! On air! "I will. Because you refuse to do it, Mike. Guess it's beneath you."

"Well, that," Mike said evenly. "Plus it's tough to get between you and sausage, so—"

"Also, you're a fatuous, pretentious idiot, so there's that."

He raised a finger. "A fatuous, pretentious idiot who *makes three times* what you do."

Everyone in the studio stared at the anchors, mouths agape in horror.

I gestured wildly to Merv. "Go to tape!" I hissed.

He held up his hands, completely at a loss. "Tape of what? End credits?"

On set, the nightmare continued.

Colleen's smile had turned dangerously brittle. "Well, that's all for this morning. See you tomorrow, folks."

"Goodbye," Mike said.

Colleen glared at him. "Goodbye," she repeated.

Oh no. Oh, no no no no no. I thought we'd resolved this.

"*Goodbye.*" Mike gave that one a cheery little brogue.

"*Goodbye!*" Colleen cried, her voice shrill.

As Merv thankfully went to credits, an assistant ran in with a phone. "It's Mr. Barnes," she explained, shoving the receiver at me. "Calling from home."

Oh, God. He'd picked *this* episode of the show to watch? I mean, *Yay, another viewer!* "Jerry?" I said uneasily into the mouthpiece.

"What the hell was that?" he bellowed.

"It was a lapse," I explained as quickly as possible. "An unfortunate lapse. I'll take care of it, I promise. I will speak to *both of them*. It will never happen again. I swear."

I turned to the set, where now, safely off the air, Colleen and Mike's bickering had taken on gale-force proportions.

Only what was the point? We were dead in the water anyway. No wonder they felt on edge. Maybe it wasn't so bad I let my staff blow off steam. Still, what Jerry said, went. After all, he still held our fate in his hands, and even if we did by some miracle meet our agreed-upon numbers, I still needed him to go to bat with me against the bigwigs.

I had every intention of keeping my word to Jerry. I would have met with Mike and Colleen right after the show, even, but I'd been stuck in meetings all day and Mike had gallivanted off to some kind of lunch fête for Tom Brokaw. So it wasn't until the next day that I was able to get the two of them into a room to hammer out their issues.

But before I even made it to the meeting, I got a special surprise: yesterday's minute-to-minutes, which featured a very noticeable bump starting as soon as the cold war between Colleen and Mike went nuclear. I stared at the sheet.

Hmmm, that was weird. Maybe it was people tuning in early for the soap opera that came on after *Daybreak*. Perhaps I should think about asking a few of the regulars onto the show to bake cookies or something. Or maybe it was the mention of Gordon Ramsay? I mean, who didn't love *Hell's Kitchen*?

That had to be it, right? There was no other reason to tune in to a morning show thirty seconds before it was over. Except . . . what was it I'd told Mike? People wanted to know his personality—they wanted to feel like he was a friend. That's why I wanted him to banter. And what if fighting was every bit as good as banter, from an entertainment perspective?

It wasn't possible, was it? But if it was true, was it worth exploring? Could I do it again?

Only this time, more so?

Why not play to our strengths? Mike was a cold, pretentious ass. Colleen was a snide, snarky queen bee. Sparks flew. People loved that shit. And what could it hurt? This was it. Eleventh hour, bottom of the ninth, fourth and goal— whatever kind of metaphor you wanted to slap on it, we had no more time and nothing to lose.

Jerry could suck it.

I met my stars on the living room set, and they were already going strong.

Colleen to Mike: "Jerk."

Mike to Colleen: "You started it."

Colleen snickered at that one. " 'You started it'? Really? Are you in kindergarten?"

I cleared my throat. "Guys, about yesterday—"

They both started talking at once. It was more of the same. I held up my hands. "*About yesterday,*" I repeated, loudly this time.

"You know," said Mike, "I don't have to sit here and be lectured by a community college dropout—"

"I'm not here to lecture you." I gave him a cool, even stare. *Your barbs have no power over me, Pomeroy.*

"You're not?" Colleen asked, baffled.

"You two are responsible professionals." That was almost the truth. "It's not for me to determine how you should behave." I looked at Colleen. "And if you want to attack him for being rude and demeaning . . ." And, sister, I was *so* there with you! I turned to Mike. "And if you feel she's utterly inadequate to perform the job at hand . . ." I shrugged. ". . . Who am I to change that? Those are your own, personal, *deeply held* beliefs. Nothing I can do."

They looked at me. They looked at each other. They looked at me. I smiled serenely.

"Good talk," I said. "Okay, show starts in a few, so . . ." I gave them two enthusiastic thumbs-up.

It was probably the cherry on the sundae. Both of my anchors looked ready to explode.

Back in the control room, Lenny greeted me. "All taken care of?"

"Oh," I said, smirking, "you betcha."

The show began, and for the first few minutes everything seemed to be business as usual. But I could see the tensions simmering beneath the surface. A few times, Colleen bit her lip. A few times, Mike gave her an almost imperceptible dirty look. We were using the living room set today, a more casual environment and one that Mike hated, since it detracted even more from his illusion of hard news. Today, I hoped that would contribute to my cause.

"Coming up in our next hour," said Colleen, "we'll be talking to people who have successfully completed an innovative rehab program." She glanced at Mike. "Might pick up some tips there."

Mike's gaze focused on her. "What I'm wondering is if they have rehab programs for angry ex–beauty queens with self-esteem issues. And if not, when are they going to start one?"

Neither of their smiles flagged for a moment.

"Coming up next after local traffic," said Colleen.

Lenny turned to me. "I thought you said—"

196

"Mmm-hmm." I steepled my hands under my chin and hid my grin.

After the break, they returned with a story on new trends in interior design.

"Wow," said Mike. "That's some butt-ugly wallpaper." The cameraman snickered.

"You're right," Colleen said. The producer on the story, standing just off set, gasped. "Reminds me a lot of your tie, actually."

Mike ran his fingers over his tie. "This is a Marinella. It's the best tie in the world. It probably cost more than your last three Botox treatments."

Lenny signaled to Merv to cut to tape.

"No," I said. "Keep going."

"Becky!" Lenny cried. "They're about to come to blows."

"You think so?" I asked hopefully. Colleen had taken that Krav Maga class last year. If Mike Pomeroy got a black eye on air . . .

The control room phone began to blink. "Ah," I said. "That'll be the illustrious Mr. Barnes." I picked it up. Yep, I was right. "Jerry," I said, "I swear, I don't know what's happening. Yes, I did speak to them. Both of them. Emphatically."

I grinned at Lenny while Jerry ranted in my ear.

"Well, I guess our option is to go straight to tape. I don't know if there's much point in anything more drastic . . . you know, considering."

"Considering you'll only be on for a few more days?" Jerry asked. "What's with you? You like *salting* the earth?"

No. But perhaps the morning television landscape could use a bit more spice.

. . .

I met Lenny at the coffee shop to, in his words, "explain what the hell is going on." I spread out several of my collected minute-to-minute records.

"On the first day," I said, pointing to the relevant numbers, "it was a tiny bump. You could see it, but barely. And it could have been a fluke, so I thought I'd try to repeat the conditions and see what happened."

He eyed me over the top of his coffee cup. "Morning television as a petri dish?"

"Exactly." I flipped a sheet. "This is yesterday. Right after the tie comment." I moved my finger down. "And then here's after he asked her if she cried ice cubes."

"Oh yeah." Lenny chuckled. "That was hilarious."

"See?" I said. "Another big spike. My theory is they love it. I think people are calling their friends during the show and telling them to turn it on every time Mike and Colleen go for the jugular."

Lenny shook his head, his mouth a thin line. "Don't you think this is a little . . . desperate?"

"Yes, maybe," I admitted. "It's desperate and weird, and sick. But also, maybe it's just that they are being real with each other instead of all fake cheery plasticine and the audience loves it. I mean, come on, Lenny. We love it."

"Yeah, but we know them. We like to see them burned a little."

"The audience feels like they know them too," I pointed out. "They've been having breakfast with them every morning. The anchors are there in their homes. They're old friends. They can deal with old friends sniping at each other. Maybe it's a thing."

Lenny didn't look convinced. "Like George and Gracie?"

"I think you'd do best not to mention that comparison to Mike and Colleen."

"Absolutely not," he agreed.

I gathered up the ratings sheets and slid them back into my folder. "It's making waves in the numbers, and that's all I need. I'll take anything. We need this. We're so close. We're almost there." I hugged the folder to my chest.

Lenny asked, "Where's 'there'?"

I froze. "You know what I mean."

"No," he said. "I don't."

"You know. Where we want . . ." I trailed off, helpless to cover for the gaffe.

"Becky, I don't know what kind of show you want to end up with here. . . ."

One that's on the air. One that continues to pay us all. "One people *watch*" was what I said out loud. And I was going to get it, even if I had to supply Mike and Colleen with their own set of switchblades and play the sound track to *West Side Story* on set.

At the next staff meeting, I got the distinct impression that my methods were contagious. The ideas people were bringing to the table had a distinctly boisterous flavor. Sasha the animal lover wanted to a do a segment on bird-catching spiders. Yes, spiders that *eat birds*. Colleen turned green. I saw green. Tracy suggested a piece on testing fabric flammability by lighting mannequins on fire.

"Why not live models?" I said.

The stage manager looked alarmed.

Dave asked about a follow-up segment on the Tampa

fraud case, and said that if pressed, he could get some of the retirees out parasailing for their interviews. I told him to book the speedboat.

"And then," I said, "we'll end the show with the segment where we get Ernie tarred and feathered in honor of the anniversary of the Boston Tea Party." That would be some red meat for our heartland viewers. I'd originally pitched it to Lisa as if it was some sort of new spa treatment. Hot mud, hot tar—same thing, right? But she hadn't gone for it and next thing I knew, she'd been "transferred" to the noon show.

So that was good.

Ernie gave a nervous laugh. "Or there's that piece on the weather vanes. It's a really good—"

"Ernie," I said.

He held his hands up in defeat. "Tarred and feathered. Got it."

"Okay, everyone!" I said. "Great meetings, great ideas. Keep 'em coming. And good show today. Thank you—"

Mike cleared his throat. We all looked at him in surprise. He hadn't talked at one of these meetings in weeks.

"Yes? Mike?" I said, eyes wide. If he said anything about the tar-and-feathering, he was next into the cauldron.

"First of all," he said, "I'd like to apologize to Colleen for my recent unprofessional behavior on the air."

Colleen's eyes widened. I exchanged a worried look with Lenny. What, was he trying to sabotage our new ratings boost? That was so Mike Pomeroy of him.

"Second, I have a story I'd like to cover. It's on . . . sauerkraut."

"Huh?" The sound came from my mouth as well as from several other spots around the table. Was "Sauerkraut" some gang of German anarchists I wasn't familiar with?

"Big annual sauerkraut festival upstate. They do bowling with cabbage, they make a big record-breaking sauerkraut cake, they have a competition for the best sauerkraut. Thought it might be good if I anchored the show from there. Change of pace."

No one said anything for a moment.

"Wow, Mike." I shook my head. "I wasn't expecting . . ."

"Local flavor. Food." Mike shrugged. "I could talk about, you know. Sauerkraut. Different flavors. Stuff like that."

"Really?" I said. "You want to cover something like—"

"You have a problem with it?"

Sauerkraut, huh? To be honest, it sounded incredibly boring, but how could I deny him. This was Mike making his own effort. He was trying to be a team player, and if sauerkraut was what it took to open him up to the idea of doing a fluff piece here and there, he could kraut it up all he wanted.

"So I can do it? Do the kraut, I mean?"

I nodded, dumbfounded. Who knew that the way to Mike Pomeroy's heart was through fermented cabbage?

After the meeting, I pounced on Lenny. "You know what this means, right?"

"That his medicine interacts poorly with scotch?" Lenny deadpanned.

"No, that I'm really getting through to him. That he *finally* sees what I'm trying to do." We left the conference room and headed down the hall toward the bullpen.

"Are you sure about that?"

We passed Mike's office. Inside, he was already hard at work making the final arrangements. "No, not Albany. The country house . . . ," he said to someone on the phone.

I waved at him. He grinned, waved back, and shut the door.

"See that?" I said in triumph. "The man loves me. We're starting to share a vision."

"Well, you *are* both a little nuts," Lenny said.

And then I had an even better idea. "I know—I'll go with him. That'll make him happy. You can be in charge of the show that day. Don't cry."

"I'll do my best," Lenny said.

"It's all very promising, right?"

"Right," said Lenny. But he didn't sound so sure.

19

The next morning, well before dawn, I waited in the darkness near Columbus Circle for the van that was supposed to take us upstate. I was, I admit, a bit concerned that Mike and his longtime cameraman, Joe, were going to ditch me. Mike hadn't sounded thrilled about the idea of me tagging along. I think he thought I was going to try to control him. But really, what sort of control did one need to exert at a kraut convention? Was he going to start interviewing hapless chefs on their feelings about Yemen or health care reform? Besides, when had I ever been able to influence Mike Pomeroy once he had a mike in his hand?

A white panel van with the IBS logo on the side pulled up to the curb. The door slid open, revealing Mike in a shirt and tie underneath his heavier hunting jacket. His suit jacket hung on a hook in the truck's main compartment, right next to all the camera equipment.

"Hey there!" I said cheerily, and climbed inside. "I brought granola bars."

"And a mix tape?" Joe asked, then snickered.

"You know you don't have to come," said Mike.

"I want to!" I cried. "Are you kidding me? You doing a story like this? I wouldn't dream of missing it."

Mike sighed. "All right, fine, whatever, blah blah blah. Let's just get on the road."

I buckled my seat belt and dug into my purse. "Okay. Peanut butter almond or mocha flax?"

The ride upstate was actually quite pleasant, as Mike and Joe reminisced about their favorite war stories from their tenures at *Nightly News*—literally, war stories. I heard about Iraqi police officers who whistled show tunes on their prison rounds and exactly what the Dalai Lama's entourage did when they weren't praying (hint: Uno).

By the time we pulled into the parking lot at the festival grounds, I was riding pretty high. I called Lenny to check in while Mike and Joe set up their establishing shots.

"We're going to open from him," I said, "and then he'll throw to Colleen. Then you can pop us back for the bumpers—"

"Is he really going to do this?" Lenny asked over the phone. He sounded even more doubtful from a distance.

"I told you," I said. "'Sharing a vision.' Ooh, they're filming the first interview. Call you right back."

Mike had crossed the lawn to one of the booths and was talking to a portly man in a stained white apron. The man was smoothing back his hair and smiling so wide I worried his face might crack in two.

"So," Mike was asking him when I got close enough to

hear. "What do you think is the secret to a really good, um, kraut?"

"Well," said the sauerkraut chef, "I would say the type of cabbage you use can really affect the kind of acidity you can create during the fermentation process. You see, you need to build up the ideal levels of the right kinds of bacteria—"

Mike cut him off. "That's terrific. Really terrific. Didn't know any of that. Well, back to you, Colleen, for . . . whatever." He smiled at the camera Joe was holding.

"And cut," said Joe, looking out from behind the viewfinder. "Yeah, that was good."

I gave him a dubious glance. Who was the producer here? "That was okay," I said. "But maybe next time you could—"

Mike and Joe, however, were already running toward the van.

"Where are you going?" I called.

"To cover the news," said Mike.

I ran to catch up with them as Jim loaded the camera gear in the car. What the hell? *This* was the news. This. Kraut.

Right?

I fixed Mike with my most executive of executive producer glowers. "Mike," I said slowly, keeping an iron grip so my tone didn't slip from pleasant to serial killer, "I am beginning to think that there's something you aren't telling me. Here, in the middle of nowhere. With a cameraman. On *Daybreak*'s dime." Mama didn't raise no fool.

"Look," Mike said, handing Joe the boom mike. "I know what you want. You want me to sit there all day like a trained monkey and do shtick for you, bickering back and forth with Colleen like Lucy and Ricky—"

Lucy and Ricky, George and Gracie, whatever. Man, there

really were no good comedy couples anymore. "Are you bickering or battling?" I asked. "Lately it's been battling, which is good for us. Think Speidi."

"Who?" he drawled.

"Spencer and Heid—"

"Don't care." He raised his hand. "As I was saying, you want me to do that while you chase ratings like some sort of crazed hamster on a wheel."

Crazed *hamster*? "Oh, come on."

"I'm done," Mike said, climbing into the van. "I'm done bickering. I'm done battling, and I'm done talking to *or* about useless celebrities with asinine combined names. If I'm going out, I'm doing it on my own terms. This morning at eight A.M. I'm going on the air with a story. A real story. A *news* story."

I stood there, silent. For a second I thought he was going to sing.

"Well?" he asked me as I stood on the grass, my heels sinking yet again into the turf. "*Are you coming with me or not?*"

"Are you kidding?" I asked, climbing in. "I'm afraid to let you out of my sight."

"I don't *know* what it is," I explained to Lenny for the fourth time.

"See, I'm not sure what that means," Lenny said. He sounded a little breathless on the other end of the line. Maybe he was pacing. If I were him, I'd have been pacing. "Is he giving you the silent treatment or something? My daughter does that."

"I mean he won't tell me." I glared at Mike, who was watching me in the rearview window. He grinned. "I mean he's kidnapped me and driven me upstate. He's rounded some sort of bend. You have to get Colleen ready with a backup story."

Mike snorted.

I rubbed my temples. "Tell Ernie . . . tell Ernie he can do his weather vanes."

"What!" Lenny cried. "No! Jesus!"

Here I was, trapped in this metal tank, headed who-knew-where, while back in Manhattan, my show went to the dogs. "What am I supposed to do?" I asked. "I need *something* to run when Mike's story tanks."

Mike snorted again.

I hung up the phone and leveled a look at him. "You are a terrible person."

"Yes, you've told me that."

"You baited me with sauerkraut. That's so low. What the hell is this story, Mike?"

"The governor," he said simply.

"What governor?" And then it all came together. His secret phone conversations. He wasn't planning a sauerkraut exposé. He was talking about that same old boring tax story he'd been hounding me about for weeks. "The financial audit shit?" I shouted. Even Joe flinched, and he apparently stood up well to mortar fire. "You're going to bury us! No one will watch that." I looked out the window. "Besides, we're nowhere near Albany."

"No, we're not." Mike turned to Joe. "Off this road here."

"Joe," I pleaded, as he steered us onto a bumpy country road. "Joe, what are you doing?"

The road gave way to a long paved driveway, at the top of which was a pretty mansion surrounded by green lawns and carefully placed shrubbery.

"Oh my God," I said, remembering more of that half-overheard conversation. "We're at the governor's country house."

"Yep." Mike and Joe started unloading the van.

"You are insane," I said to him. "You are experiencing a psychotic break and I *won't* be dragged down with you. I refuse."

"Suit yourself," said Mike. "You can stay by the car. Joe, ready?"

"You can't just go up there with a camera. You're going to get us both arrested . . . and *fired*. If I get fired, I never work again, you lunatic!"

Mike slipped on his suit jacket, checked his hair in the van's side mirror, and started up the hill, Joe and his camera following behind.

"I'm not going to run it!" I called. "You can't make me run it! I'll run live coverage of Colleen getting a bikini wax first!"

And she'd do that for me too. Colleen was a pro. Unlike this certifiable madman. He was still going. He didn't care.

"Mike!" I screamed at the top of my lungs. "They're going to cancel the show!"

Now he turned and looked at me. Joe did the same.

"If we don't get our numbers up by the end of this week, we're toast. They're going to replace us with sitcoms and game shows on reruns."

At last. At last it was out there. I almost collapsed from relief. Mike's expression softened just a tad as he stared back at me, small and tired and holding things together with duct tape and prayer.

He had to understand. *Come on, Mike.* Another news outlet biting the dust? Surely he cared about *that*.

And then he turned back around and starting ascending the drive.

Oh, did I hate him! I hated Mike Pomeroy. I rued the day I first saw him on the evening news. I cursed the moment I got the idea to hire him. I denounced any vestigial scraps of my childhood crush.

I pulled out my cell and called Lenny. "Are you ready to go?" I asked him. "I need you to be ready in case . . ."

"What the hell is going on?"

Now in front of the door, Mike checked his watch and scanned the lawn. "You'll know when to go live," he said to me.

"Go live with what?" I asked him. I nearly gave him the finger. Into the phone, I said, "Lenny, I need those weather vanes. I need 'em, I need 'em."

"Please, no," said Lenny.

Mike checked his watch one more time, then rang the doorbell. A moment later, Governor Willis answered. He looked rested and relaxed, a smile on his face, a cup of coffee in his hand. Might as well have been a campaign poster.

"Pomeroy!" he called with a smile. "What the hell are you doing here?" They shook hands jovially. Probably another one of Mike's old drinking buddies.

"Becky?" said Lenny in my ear. "We're almost ready. Colleen's in place and we . . . um, we have the weather vanes."

I watched Mike talking to Willis. He hadn't brought a cameraman here to chat about scotch, that was for sure. And not even Mike Pomeroy was going to interrupt the governor's breakfast to discuss something as boring as an audit. What did he have up his sleeve?

"Becky?" Lenny asked. "Am I running it? Becky?"

"Gary," Mike said to the governor. "I wanted to know how you felt about a few things. . . ."

"Uh, okay." The governor seemed good-natured but confused to find Mike on his porch in anchorman wear.

"I need to know in ten seconds," Lenny said, now frantic. "*Ten seconds*, Becky!"

"All right," I said. "Do it."

"Run the weather vanes?" Lenny asked.

"Yes. I—no. Wait. Just wait a second." Because Mike Pomeroy was *on* right now. Kosovo on. Condoleezza Rice on. Hurricane Katrina on. I knew that look, and not just from TV. It was the look in his eyes when he'd shot that pheasant. It was the look of a predator about to pounce.

"Specifically," Mike said, like a pitcher winding up, "I'd like to know how you feel about the fact that the attorney general is filing charges against you for racketeering, for steering government contracts to your relatives and cronies."

Willis gave an uneasy laugh. "Mike, I don't know where you get your information."

"Not to mention the money laundering," Mike said as if he hadn't heard him.

Lenny was still shouting in my ear, but it was like I heard him through a great fog. "We're coming back from break. Five, four, three—"

Mike leaned against he doorjamb, cool as an icy drink. "And you can tell me: There's a hooker or two in there also, isn't there, Gary?"

Oh my God. This was news. This was real *real* news.

"BECKY!" Lenny yelled.

"Live!" I screamed into the phone. "Live! We're going live now! *Come to me right now!*"

20

"What?" cried Lenny.

"*Now*, Lenny!" I shouted myself hoarse. "*Now now now now now!*"

I heard Lenny give the command and held my breath.

Turns out, I needn't have worried.

Willis motioned to the camera. "You know I like you, Mike, but if you don't leave, I'm calling the police."

"Oh," said Mike, "I don't think you'll need to do that." Which was when I heard the sirens. I turned, along with Joe and the watchful eye of his camera, to see a string of police cars headed up the drive.

"Shit!" Governor Willis yelled, and slammed the door shut. The officers swarmed from their cars and fanned out over the yard, running to the back of the house. Mike gave the play-by-play as the situation unfolded.

My heart was in my throat as I watched events unfurl with the kind of drama I was used to seeing only with a chyron obscuring part of the view. I was watching news. Real news. Real news read by Mike "fucking" Pomeroy. Holy cow.

In a few moments, it was all over. They'd caught Willis and were leading him away in handcuffs. Joe framed the shot so we could see Willis being taken to the car while Mike talked to the camera.

"Federal authorities had been planning the raid for weeks. This reporter has learned that the indictment lists fifteen counts of racketeering and using undue influence. Sources tell me prosecutors have taped phone calls as well as incriminating emails. . . ."

Lenny called again. "We're all speechless back here, boss," he said to me.

"I know the feeling." I shook my head in wonderment at my anchorman. Mike Pomeroy, ladies and gentlemen. The most legendary newsman alive.

And when the broadcast was done, and half a dozen news crews had arrived on the scene to do cleanup duty, we walked together in silence back down the drive toward the van.

"You could have just told me about this," I said to him at last. "I might have covered it anyway."

"Liar," said Mike.

"How'd you do it?"

"There was a little item in that upstate newspaper about the governor's taxes. You know, the one you blew off?"

I nodded.

"I called my contacts at the IRS and found out that the FBI had pulled all the governor's returns. Then I called some people over at the Bureau, but they kind of clammed up. So then I talked to my friends at the State Senate, who told me a special committee was being impaneled for Monday."

"Wow," I said. He'd just put my entire network of Jersey contacts to shame. Of course, he had a few decades on me.

"So I called car dispatch at NYFBI and asked what day this week they were sending out any teams of more than three cars." He shrugged. "Basically, I had a hunch, and it took about a month to shake out."

I stared at him, deeply impressed. Maybe if I paid close attention to him, I'd win a Pulitzer one day too.

"Look," he said to me. "I get it. I know no one cares about what it means to do this job. But I'm not here to read copy. I'm an investigative journalist. I can do that. And I wanted you to see it."

Oh, I saw it. I saw it and I was right back to worshipping at his feet. Jerk or no. Pain in my ass or no. Mike Pomeroy was a news god.

"It's a great story, Mike," I said, trying to keep the reverence out of my voice. Which wasn't too difficult, since, after all, I knew his other side now. "More than a great story. Great television, too. It was . . . bran . . . but with a donut. A bran donut!"

He laughed. "You're a weird one, fangirl."

We reached the van. Joe had already packed up the camera equipment and had gone to bum a cigarette off someone from CBS. We leaned against the open cargo step and watched the circus go on without us. As the adrenaline ebbed, I started feeling the chill of the morning mountain air. I was shocked that my BlackBerry wasn't ringing off the hook yet. I wondered how many of the news programs were running our footage of Willis's attempted escape. Mike's footage.

I sneaked a peek at my anchor. He seemed relaxed now, and definitely a little smug as he watched the other, younger newscasters hoofing it up the hill to give their Johnny-come-lately reports. I smiled. Mike Pomeroy may have had a few years on today's talking heads, but that just meant he was light-years ahead of them when it came to talent.

Perhaps I could afford to be a little smug myself. After all, I'd been the one to recognize it in him.

After a while, Mike spoke again. "So I have that one grandkid," he said. "From the picture?"

"Yeah?"

"His name is Alexander. My daughter lives on the Upper West Side with her husband and her son—with Alexander. I haven't seen them since I got fired from *Nightly News*."

I stiffened, stunned by this information.

"First I was embarrassed," he said. "And then, when I got back on TV . . . well, after all I'd accomplished, to be forced to come back like *this*."

If he'd been getting naked right there in front of me, I wouldn't have been more shocked.

"Truth is," he admitted, "I'd screwed things up with my kids long before I was canned, anyway. I was never at home, and even when I was, I was answering every phone call, watching TV out of the corner of my eye all the time."

I took a deep breath. That sounded far too familiar.

"My marriage failed," he said. "And then another. You know how it is."

"No," I replied. "I've never been married."

"Yeah well, you're even worse than me. You'd *sleep* in the office if you could."

"I've got more monitors there, yes," I said with a rueful laugh.

But Mike wasn't laughing. "Let me skip ahead for you. I'll tell you how this all turns out: You end up with nothing. And that's what I had before you showed up."

It was like he'd punched me in the stomach. I turned to face him, but he wasn't quite meeting my eyes.

"So . . . what I meant to say was . . . thank you." He nodded with finality and looked up at me.

"Wait a second," I said coyly. "Did you just say something nice?"

"Told you I could banter." And then I saw Mike Pomeroy's real smile. Not the rictus mask he'd wear on the show whenever we told him to act cheerful, but his actual smile. It was a little lopsided, but intensely charming. Nice counterpoint to the silver hair and the gravelly voice. Unexpected, and welcome.

I wrapped my arms around myself and squeezed. "So should we head back?"

He grabbed his coat off the back of the passenger seat and draped it over my shoulders. "Sure. I'll round up Joe."

I wrinkled my nose. The jacket had a decidedly gamy odor. "Mike," I whined. "Is this where you put your pheasants?"

We were welcomed back at the IBS building like soldiers coming home from the war; I was surprised there wasn't a ticker tape parade on the plaza. Ernie was the only one who seemed less than thrilled about our last-minute live broadcast, and I was in such a good mood, I might have offered to do his segment on the weather vanes.

A little drunk on our victory, I went up to Jerry's office as soon as the ratings came in.

"What do you think?" I asked him.

"They're not . . . awful," he said.

Damned right they weren't awful. They were actually phenomenal. I perched on the edge of his desk. "So how much longer can we get?"

"With these . . ." He tapped his pencil against the sheet. "A year. A pretty comfortable year."

I giggled, then clapped my hand over my mouth. I'd done it! Or, um, Mike had done it. But still. Mike had been my idea, so . . .

Jerry shook his head as he regarded me. "I underestimated you, Becky."

"That is so true."

He cleared his throat. "NBC called. They want to know how much time you have left on your contract."

"What?" I slipped off the side of the desk and barely saved myself from going *splat* on his carpet.

"The *Today* show wants you."

"WHAT?" I repeated, inanely. The *Today* show? Maybe I *had* gone *splat* on the carpet. Maybe I'd bashed my head open and was hallucinating all of this. "You're kidding."

"I'm not." He frowned. "And now I'm wishing we had a real contract with you. Just in case."

I tried to give my best casual laugh. I'm not sure I was particularly convincing. Still, I'm proud to report that I made it out the door before I started my victory dance.

But I couldn't celebrate. Not for real. Not yet. So while the rest of the *Daybreak* staff went out to party triumphantly over finally being taken seriously in the building, I headed straight to Schiller's. Adam was there with his friends, as usual. God, he looked good.

After a moment, he saw me. I waved. He looked down into his drink. I almost turned and bolted, but then he sighed, put down his beer, and came over.

"Outside to talk?" I suggested.

"Yeah," he said. "Think so."

On the street, I launched into my prepared apology without preamble. "I was wrong," I said. "I was scared. I was stupid. And I was a coward."

Adam blinked at my confession, but his gaze didn't soften. "More," he said. "I think there was something more you wanted to say."

There was. There was much more. But this would do for a start. I took a deep breath. "I made myself believe you were every person that's sailed past me in my life. That you were going to dismiss me, or make light of me. But that's not you, Adam. You're . . . good and strong and kind. Not to mention really skilled at charades."

He thought about it for a moment. "That's not bad."

Another deep breath. "They were going to cancel the show."

His lips parted in surprise.

"Yeah. I couldn't tell anyone. That's why I've been doing what I've been doing. That's why I've been so desperate. But somehow, through some crazy mix of hard work and low inhibitions and really good luck, we saved it." I laughed. I still couldn't believe it. "But the thing is, the second I knew everything was okay, the person I wanted to tell was you."

And now he smiled.

"Because the thing is . . . because I didn't really believe in myself before, I was afraid of what you'd think if you discovered that I was a failure. That I'd destroyed the show. But now, now that I haven't, now that I actually have a future, what I really want is to know that you're proud of me. Is that crazy?"

"No," said Adam. "It's the only thing that makes sense." And then suddenly we were in each other's arms, and I knew exactly how right he was.

We celebrated at Schiller's. We celebrated with an after-cocktails dinner. And then we headed back to Adam's house for even more celebrating.

As we grappled our way toward his bedroom, ripping off clothes as we went, I marveled that not once that evening had I thought about turning on the news. Maybe Mike was right and I needed to find a little balance, before I lost it all.

"What time is it?" I asked Adam. "Midnight?"

He chuckled. "I think it's closer to nine."

"Nine!" I exclaimed. "Oh my God it's late!"

A second later, I heard my BlackBerry go off from inside my jacket pocket. I jumped off Adam and scurried out of the bedroom, clad only in my shirt. Now, let's see. Where did my blazer go flying? I padded around the floor, searching for my clothes in the dark.

"Not again!" Adam yelled from the bedroom.

"Just a minute!" I called back. Ah, there it was. I snatched up the phone, walked into the kitchen . . .

And threw it in the fridge.

The next morning, happy with my show, happy with my man, happy with Mike, happy with the world, I paraded around my office, giving orders and feeling the love. I met with Mike to brief him on our plans for next week.

"So tomorrow we're doing the Supreme Court justice hearings at the top of the hour."

"Great," said Mike, making a note of it.

"Oh," I added. "Anthony Bourdain called. He wants to come on and do a segment with you about—"

"Bourdain?" said Mike. "Love him. Not doing that."

I furrowed my brow. Huh? *Not* doing it? I couldn't have heard him correctly.

"But say hi to Tony for me," Mike added. "I owe him a bottle of Patrón."

I gaped at him. "So you're saying you're *friends* with this guy but you won't appear on your show with him?"

"That's it, fangirl." Mike slapped his hand against his notebook. "Come now. We did one good story together and now you think I'm your sidekick? Sorry. Don't think so."

I let out an indignant gasp as he started to walk away. "Wait!" I called. "I saved your life, remember? Or was that all just bullshit? You can't do a couple of stories for me?"

He didn't turn around; he didn't even *fucking* turn around. I couldn't believe it. I didn't think last week meant the world to us, but I didn't think it had meant nothing, either. I'd let him have his story! I'd praised him for his hard work! I didn't want a sidekick, I wanted some goddamned *respect*. I was his executive producer and he was acting like he did me a favor every time he spoke on camera.

I shook my head. "What is wrong with me?" I asked no one in particular. "What am I doing here, beating my head against the wall for? I could go to the *Today* show, where you don't have to poke Matt Lauer with a stick to get him to eat a donut or two."

Now he stopped. "The *Today* show?"

Yes, you pompous ass! You're not the only bit of talent around this show. "They offered me a job—"

"Of course they did," he muttered.

I lifted my chin. "But I said—"

"—Time to trade up?" Mike suggested.

"I said *no*, you paranoid mule." Jesus, what a drama queen. No wonder he'd ended up in *front* of the camera.

But Mike was already well into his tirade. "I don't know why I trusted you. All that awful enthusiasm and the bullshit about me being your idol—"

"Did you not hear me?" I railed. "*I said no*. But God, what if I *did* go? Could anyone blame me, really? Come on, Mike. If you had *ever* done *one thing* I asked, made *one S'more*, anything—"

"You don't care about this job!" he cried. "You only care about grabbing every brass ring, climbing every ladder. What's enough for you, Becky Fuller? News president? Network president? *Santa Claus?*"

You know what would have been enough for me? A tiny bit of gratitude that I'd put him back at a news desk. A dash of team player attitude when I asked him to talk to Taylor Swift or Tim Gunn. A soupçon of respect for the idea that morning shows, fluff and all, actually did offer something of value to their audience.

Adam could give me that, and he produced serious news stories. Why couldn't Mike offer the same amount of professional courtesy? And you know what? Adam had even warned me about this, sometime in the middle of all the celebrating last night. I'd just been too high on life to believe him. I'd told him about *Today,* and I'd told him I wasn't leaving IBS, and he said that maybe I shouldn't be so hasty.

I'd chalked up his reticence to his lingering hatred for Mike Pomeroy. But once again, Adam was right.

Enough of this bullshit. I was better than this, and NBC, at least, recognized that.

"You want to hear something *really* ridiculous? Until ten seconds ago, I had actually decided to turn my back on the best job I'd ever be offered. Isn't that absurd?"

"Yes," Mike agreed. "Go. What's stopping you? *Go.*"

I clenched my jaw and my fists. How could he say all this to me, after the governor's house? I could barely form a coherent sentence, I was so upset. "If you had ever—ever treated me with some loyalty and trust and friendship— things you seem *incapable* of . . . I would be leaving in spite of you, not *because* of you, you miserable, selfish, lonely, egotistical asshole!"

I stopped, breathing hard. I couldn't believe the string of insults that had just shot out of my mouth.

Neither, apparently, could Mike, as he turned and stalked off. But I wasn't left alone. No, everyone was staring at me now. Lenny, Colleen, Merv, Sasha, Tracy, Dave—the entire *Daybreak* family had just heard my outburst.

Well, at least this time they hadn't caught it on camera.

One of the interns came running down the hall. "Oh, hey, Becky!" she said, and leaned close. "You have a call. It's the *Today* show."

Perfect. Perfect timing, too.

21

The next morning at eight sharp, I walked through the front doors of 30 Rockefeller Plaza. NBC. I was wearing my nicest suit, my finest heels. My hair was perfect, my makeup understated. I was interviewing at the *Today* show. They were going to headhunt me right out of IBS.

And I couldn't wait. Screw Mike Pomeroy. He had no idea what he'd just lost.

I met with two executives in their conference room, a gorgeous space with polished tables and a bank of monitors on the far wall. It was like Becky Fuller heaven. Every monitor showed a different morning show. Half a dozen cheery hosts and hostesses greeting the day and their audience. There, at the bottom right corner, was *Daybreak*.

"We want the show to have that real youthful energy," said one of the executives.

"You've done such an amazing job of revitalizing *Daybreak*," said the other.

"Thanks," I said, dragging my eyes off the *Daybreak* monitor. "I appreciate that. And it's . . . it's really great to be here."

Behind the second executive's head, Mike and Colleen were arguing. As usual. It was amazing—you could actually see the increased dynamism between my two hosts as they tore each other to shreds.

I wondered what they were saying today. I hoped Colleen was getting him good. She looked like she was, at least, if his thundercloud of a face was anything to go by. Good. The Asshole deserved it. I wished them many long years of ratings-boosting battles.

Actually, strike that. I hoped the *Today* show ratings smashed them to smithereens. Maybe then Mike would realize how valuable I'd been to him. I mean, would anyone else have even put his governor story on the air? Would any other producer have trusted him enough to make that call? I know Adam wouldn't have. Too much bullshit, too much water under the bridge. I was the only one who'd still believed in Mike. Shame he didn't believe in me.

"We'd like to get you aboard as soon as possible," said the first exec. Right—the interview.

"Oh, great!" I said, trying to turn away from the *Daybreak* screen and focus. "Um . . ." Okay, that was weird. Mike had just stormed off the set. "Sorry," I said, distracted. "It's just . . . usually this segment is a two-shot with Colleen and Mike but . . . Mike's not there."

They looked at me stupidly.

"Never mind!" I said, my tone cheery. "They must have changed it. Anyway, sorry. You were saying?"

"We wanted to ask you what your plans are for sports coverage," said the second exec, clearly taken aback by my inability to pay attention to their offer.

"Right," I said. "Sports coverage." Okay, something exceedingly weird was happening on *Daybreak*. Someone had taken a handheld camera and was following Mike down the hall to the Craft Services table. We'd been very careful not to take the cameras backstage; we didn't need anyone seeing the kind of conditions we worked in. But there they were, in our cluttered hallways, zooming in on our scuffed folding tables as Mike gathered up a bunch of food. What the hell?

The NBC people were eyeing me suspiciously.

"Right," I said. "So, um, with respect to sports coverage, I think we should reach out to women through their kids. It's not that big a step from being a soccer mom to being a real fan—oh my God, what are they doing?"

The executives turned around. On-screen, I saw the *Daybreak* kitchen set. And in front of the stove, tying on an apron . . . was Mike Pomeroy.

I grabbed a remote off the table. "Sorry," I said, turning up the volume. "Hope you don't mind. Hey, Mike Pomeroy has a nervous breakdown on set, that's news, right?"

Mike cracked a few eggs into a bowl. "Thought we'd change things up a bit today," he said, starting to whisk.

I stared at the screen, my mouth a perfect O.

"In the fifteen hundreds," he said, "the Italians invented a meal for their afternoon repast. Something they could make using the ingredients they had available."

"Holy shit," I whispered. I didn't care that all the NBC execs were staring at me. I didn't care that I'd probably just blown this interview. Mike Pomeroy was cooking. On the air.

"I've been making frittatas for about twenty years," he

224

said, adding in some chopped veggies he must have stolen off the crudités platter from Craft Services. "Ever since I was taught how on a naked weekend with an Italian movie star who shall go unnamed." He winked at the screen. "Occasionally, I make them at home. But only for people—only for people I really care about."

I dropped back into my seat.

"The key to a frittata," Mike told the camera, "is to use a really hot pan. Because that, my friends, is what makes it"— he paused dramatically—"*fluffy*."

I cracked up laughing. The executives all turned to me, bewildered.

"Sorry," I said, still chuckling. "It's an inside—sorry." And so much better than "flocculent." That would have made the frittata sound diseased.

My BlackBerry began to buzz. I pulled it out of my pocket. Adam.

"Are you watching this?" he asked when I answered.

"Yes." I nodded, blown away. "He said 'fluffy.' On air."

"I *know*." Adam paused. "What are you going to do?"

I looked at the executives. At the beautiful desk. At the opportunity I was about to destroy.

"He's not going to ask you twice," Adam said.

Deep breath. "Sorry, guys," I said to NBC. "I gotta go."

I started running the second I cleared the elevator. The streets were packed with morning commuters, and I jostled my way through the throng, ducking slow-moving tourists, racing against the lights, playing chicken with taxicabs. I raced down Sixth Avenue, cut through back alleys and arcades, kicked off my shoes, and sprinted through Bryant Park—and there, at the IBS plaza, on the big screen, I could see Mike. He was still making his breakfast. He was still explaining to the world exactly how you're supposed to flip a frittata.

I hurried through the lobby and into the elevator. I ran through the tangled hallways of the *Daybreak* offices and burst out onto the edge of the set. Mike was just pulling his completed, perfect, *fluffy* frittata out of the oven.

"Now you have to let it cool a bit," he was saying. Of course. Because frittatas were eaten at room temperature. I remembered.

Everyone was standing there, staring at Mike with the kind of awe that I was feeling. Colleen's mouth was open. Lenny had gone white. Even Adam was there, watching the proceedings with a disbelieving smile.

Mike looked up from his work and caught sight of me.

"Later this week," he said, "I'll show you how to make fantastic beignets. Or, as the rabble like to call them"—he smiled at me: his real smile—"donuts."

I threw back my head and laughed.

Adam came over to me. "You know, he's still the third-worst—"

"Oh," I said. "I know it."

Colleen approached next. "No NBC?"

I shook my head.

"Good, because it was nice to finally have a decent producer around here." She studied Mike in his apron; he looked surprisingly in his element there on the kitchen set. "Oh, and Gidget? I want a tropical fruit plate."

On Anna's first morning at *Daybreak,* I presented her with her very own gift bag. She gave me a coy smile, then pulled out a T-shirt. The front read: WELCOME TO DAYBREAK. The back? OH, FUUUUUUUUUU—

"I love it!" cried Anna. She threw her arms around me. I sent her over to Sasha and Tracy to get settled in, then surveyed my domain. On top of new doorknobs, we'd gotten a new sound system and an upgrade to our set. Things were bustling: Merv and Lenny going over some of the shots, the producers and stage managers scooting around. I saw Colleen and Mike walking down the hall together—and Mike being totally unsubtle about the way he placed his hand on Colleen's rear end.

Yeah, that was going to be one hot mess when it went south. I could only cross my fingers and hope their on-air battles were the better for it. But I didn't want to obsess over that now. I caught him before he disappeared into her dressing room.

"Hey, Mike," I said. "Come take a quick walk with me before the show. Come on," I coaxed. "Real quick."

On the plaza, I grabbed a copy of the *New York Post* from one of the vendors and turned to Page Six. "Listen to this: 'His gravity leavens the silliness of morning TV, making an incongruous but somehow perfect match.'"

Mike rolled his eyes, but I kept reading. He might not like the idea of rave reviews of his "performance," but I did, and so did the IBS execs.

"'It turns out,'" I went on as we strolled down the plaza, "'that after forty years in the TV news business, the real Mike Pomeroy has finally arrived.' Not bad, huh?"

He nodded, then spoke again. "By the way, I'm getting my prostate checked next week. I thought I might take a crew with me—"

I clapped my hands with excitement. "That's a great idea!"

Mike shook his head. "Jesus, I was *kidding*."

"Seriously, though," I said, "it would be a real public health message. And they have these little cameras now that go right up your—"

"*No.*"

"Aww, come on, Mike . . . ," I said as we walked off together, into the sunrise.

About the Author

DIANA PETERFREUND is the author of *Secret Society Girl*, *Under the Rose*, *Rites of Spring (Break)*, and *Tap & Gown*. She has also published two fantasy novels for teens about killer unicorns: *Rampant* and *Ascendant*, as well as several short stories. She was raised in Florida, graduated from Yale University with degrees in geology and literature, and worked as a journalist and food critic before turning to fiction. Diana Peterfreund lives in Washington, D.C., with her husband.

About the Screenwriter

In 2006, ALINE BROSH McKENNA wrote the screen adaptation of *The Devil Wears Prada*, garnering her nominations for the WGA, BAFTA, and Scripter Awards. In 2008, she wrote the original screenplay *27 Dresses*. She also shares credit on the romantic comedies *Three to Tango* and *Laws of Attraction*.

McKenna recently adapted Benjamin Mee's memoir *We Bought a Zoo*, which Cameron Crowe is attached to direct. Currently, she is writing a new version of *Cinderella* for Disney.

McKenna is a magna cum laude graduate of Harvard University. After graduation, she moved to New York where she co-wrote the book *A Coed's Companion* for Pocketbooks. In a summer film class at NYU, she wrote her first screenplay, which she sold to New Regency Productions.

McKenna lives in Los Angeles with her husband and two children.